2024

Training Quali

Original-Prüfungsaufgaben

Bayern

Englisch

LÖSUNGEN

STARK

© 2023 Stark Verlag GmbH
18. ergänzte Auflage
www.stark-verlag.de

Inhalt

Musteraufgabe und Original-Prüfungsaufgaben

Sobald die Lösungen der Original-Prüfungsaufgaben 2023 freigegeben sind, können sie als **PDF** auf der Plattform **MyStark** heruntergeladen werden (vgl. Code auf der Umschlaginnenseite vorne im Buch).

Autorin: Birgit Mohr

Vorwort

Liebe Schülerin, lieber Schüler,

dieses Buch enthält die Lösungen zu dem Band **Training Quali Englisch Bayern** (Bestellnummer: D09350).
Die Lösungen bzw. Lösungsvorschläge in diesem Buch ermöglichen es dir, deine Leistung einzuschätzen. Im Aufgabenband ist am Rand jeweils angegeben, auf welchen Seiten du die Lösungen in diesem Lösungsband findest. Durch die **Hinweise** zu einzelnen Aufgaben lernst du auch, was bei einer bestimmten Aufgabenstellung von dir erwartet wird.

Viel Erfolg im Quali wünscht dir

Birgit Mohr

Übungsaufgaben
Lösungen zum „Hör- und Hörsehverstehen“

Allgemeiner Hinweis: *Zum Lösen aller folgenden Aufgaben zum Kapitel „Hör- und Hörsehverstehen“ musst du dir den Text jeweils genau anhören. Wenn du ihn nach dem ersten Hören noch nicht verstanden hast, kannst du ihn dir natürlich auch öfter anhören. Lies dir den Hörverstehenstext nur durch, wenn du bei den Lösungen unsicher bist und gar nicht weiterkommst.*

TEST 1: In the supermarket

Dear customers, welcome to Richie's Supermarket, where you can always get a bargain!
This week we are celebrating health week at Richie's Supermarket, and we take special care to offer you the best products for the health of your whole family at the best prices you can find!
In our fruit and vegetable department, you can pick your choice of the best apples, pears or tomatoes for just 59 pence per kilo! Yes, that's one kilo of apples, pears or tomatoes for just 59 pence! By the way, the 5 kilogram bag of potatoes now costs only 1 pound 79.
Or, if you are looking for some relaxing moments, why don't you visit our cosmetics department, where you will find a wide selection of natural bath products for just 99 pence each. Imagine, you can take a refreshing, relaxing bath, with the fragrance of your choice, for just 99 pence! What's more, all sun lotions are now reduced by 25 %.
Dear customers, at Richie's Supermarket we care for your health. Take your time to find out about our offers, and enjoy your health week with us!

Aufgabe 1

a) Richie's
   Hinweis: *Z. 1*

b) health week
   Hinweis: *Z. 3*

Aufgabe 2

a) 59 pence
   Hinweis: *Z. 6 f.*

b) 1 pound 79 pence
   Hinweis: *Z. 8 f.*

c) 99 pence
   Hinweis: *Z. 11 f.*

d) 25 %
   Hinweis: *Z. 13 f.*

Aufgabe 3

a) *wrong:* protests, *correct:* products

b) *wrong:* friend, *correct:* fruit

c) *wrong:* normal, *correct:* natural

d) *wrong:* money, *correct:* time

TEST 2: At the airport

Part 1: At the check-in

Mr Miller: Good afternoon, my wife and I have tickets to Munich. I hope we are not too late for the flight.

Woman at service desk: Please give me your tickets and your passports.

Mr Miller: Here they are.

Woman at service desk: Thank you. OK, let me check …

Woman at service desk: Mr and Mrs Miller – you are going to Munich via Frankfurt?

Mr Miller: Yes, we have to change planes in Frankfurt.

Woman at service desk: OK, you are still on time for the flight to Frankfurt. But you have to hurry – the plane is going to take off in 20 minutes! Where would you like to sit in the plane, by the window or on the aisle?

Mr Miller: On the aisle, please.

Woman at service desk: No problem. I am giving you two seats in the centre row – one of them is next to the aisle. Would you like to check in any luggage?

Mr Miller: No, thanks, we have only hand luggage.

Woman at service desk: OK.

Woman at service desk: Here are your boarding cards to Frankfurt, and from Frankfurt to Munich. Please proceed to Gate 17 immediately.

Mr Miller: Thank you.

Woman at service desk: Enjoy your flight!

Aufgabe 1

a) true
Hinweis: *Z. 2*

b) false
Hinweis: *Z. 4 f.*

c) false
Hinweis: *Z. 13*

d) false
Hinweis: *Z. 16*

Aufgabe 2

a) their tickets and passports
Hinweis: *Z. 4*

b) in Frankfurt
Hinweis: *Z. 9*

c) in 20 minutes
Hinweis: *Z. 11*

d) 17
Hinweis: *Z. 19*

Part 2: Boarding the plane

(Busy sounds of passengers boarding the plane)

Woman: Excuse me, sir?

Mr Miller: Who? Me?

Woman: Yes, sir. Excuse me, I'm sorry to bother you but it looks like you are sitting in my seat.

Mr Miller: Oh, really? Let me check our boarding cards …

(Rustling in his travel bag.)

Mr Miller: Hmm, where are they … just a moment.

Woman: Sure, no hurry.

Mr Miller: Ah, here they are. Let me just check … Here, please take a look, my wife and I have seats 21D and 21E. Which seat do you have?

Woman: Oops, that's strange. My seat number is 21E, too!

Mr Miller: This is very strange. It must be the airline's mistake!

Woman *(sighing)*: It must be! Wait a moment, I'm just going to ask the flight attendant.

(Some time passes.)

Flight attendant: Hello, sir! This lady tells me that you have the same seat as she does. Could you please show me your boarding cards?

Mr Miller: Yes, of course. Here, these are the boarding cards for my wife and myself.

Flight attendant: 21D and 21E … Mr and Mrs Miller … The flight number and date are correct. You really are sitting in the right seat. Could you show me your boarding card again, please?

Woman: OK, here it is.

Flight attendant: Ah, that's it! This boarding card is for another flight. Look, it has the same flight number, but the date was two weeks ago! Did you travel to Frankfurt two weeks ago, too?

Woman: Oh, yes, you're right, excuse me. This is my fault, it's the wrong boarding card. I travel to Frankfurt every two weeks and that's an old one. Let me just check in my bag …

Flight attendant: No problem for you, Mr and Mrs Miller, you have the right seats.

Mr Miller: OK, thank you.

Woman: I'm afraid I can't find my boarding card, I don't know where I put it.

Flight attendant: That's no problem. Please come with me and I will look up your seat on the computer. *(Voice fading)* It's not the first time that somebody lost their boarding card on the way from the gate to the plane …

Aufgabe 3

a) B

Hinweis: *Z. 5 f.*

b) A

Hinweis: *Z. 14*

c) C

Hinweis: *Z. 21 f.*

d) C

Hinweis: *Z. 25*

e) B

Hinweis: *Z. 33*

Aufgabe 4

a) 21E

b) (the) boarding card(s)

c) 2/two weeks before/ago

d) (on the) computer

TEST 3: Mrs Brown at the shoe store

Part 1

Shop assistant: Hello, how can I help you?

Mrs Brown: Hello, I'm looking for a pair of shoes for the summer.

Shop assistant: Do you have something specific in mind?

Mrs Brown *(hesitantly)*: Mm, yes. I'd like a pair of comfortable leather shoes.

Shop assistant: What colour are you looking for?

Mrs Brown: A light colour please, maybe white or beige.

Shop assistant: OK, please come over to our summer section.

Aufgabe 1

a) summer
   Hinweis: *Z. 3*

b) comfortable
   Hinweis: *Z. 5*

c) beige
   Hinweis: *Z. 7*

Part 2

Shop assistant: Here, take a look at this pair. They are a new design from Italy and are very comfortable. Are these the type of shoes you like to wear?

Mrs Brown: Not exactly. These shoes are too high – I don't think I could wear them for more than an hour. I also don't like it that my toes show. I'd like a closed pair of shoes that I can wear with socks.

Shop assistant: Of course. Please come over to this aisle, where we have the more casual shoes.

Shop assistant *(after a moment)*: Here, please have a look. What do you think of these loafers, which are a nice beige? These are from another collection from Italy.

Mrs Brown: Oh, yes, they do look nice! I think I'd like to try them.

Shop assistant: What size can I get for you?

Mrs Brown: That would be a 5, thank you.

Aufgabe 2

a) toes
   Hinweis: *Z. 5*

b) socks
Hinweis: *Z. 6*

c) Italy
Hinweis: *Z. 10 ff.*

Part 3

Shop assistant: How do the shoes fit? Do they feel comfortable?

Mrs Brown: Phew, I'm afraid they don't fit. Have you got them half a size larger?

Shop assistant: One moment, I'll go to the back again to look. I'm not sure that we still have this style in 5 ½, I think we've already sold all of them. *(pause while he goes to look)*

Mrs Brown: And, have you got them in 5 ½?

Shop assistant: Sorry, I'm afraid not. Size 5 ½ is completely sold out. But I did bring you a size 6. Would you like to have a try?

Mrs Brown: Oh, that's a pity ... but OK, I'll try them.

Mrs Brown *(after a moment)*: Let's see ...

Shop assistant: What do you think, do they fit nicely?

Mrs Brown: Yes, I think they do fit! But I'm a bit surprised that I'm a size 6 now!

Shop assistant: Don't worry, this make is sometimes a bit tighter than others.

Mrs Brown: OK ... Well, I've made up my mind – I would like to buy these shoes.

Shop assistant: Perfect!

Aufgabe 3

a) fit
Hinweis: *Z. 3*

b) 5.5/5 ½
Hinweis: *Z. 3 ff.*

c) 6
Hinweis: *Z. 13 ff.*

Part 4

Girl at cash register: Hello, how are you today? What would you like to pay for?

Mrs Brown: That pair of beige loafers, please.

Girl at cash register: OK.

Girl at cash register: That'll be forty-nine ninety-five. Would you like to pay by cash or credit card?

Mrs Brown: I'd like to pay by credit card, please. Here you are.

Girl at cash register: Thanks!

Girl at cash register: So, here are your shoes. Thanks very much. Goodbye now.
Mrs Brown: Thanks. Goodbye!

Aufgabe 4

a) true
 Hinweis: *Z. 3*

b) false
 Hinweis: *Z. 5*

c) true
 Hinweis: *Z. 7*

TEST 4: Visit to Stirling Castle

Part 1
(Conversation starts between two teenagers on back seat of a car)

Tabby: Nick, you've been playing that game for hours now, could you please turn it off?

Nick *(sounding absent)*: No.

Tabby: Nick, please! I don't want to hear that sound anymore. Could you turn it off, now!?

Nick *(concentrating on his game)*: Sorry, Tabby, I can't turn it off, now ... I have to finish this level first.

Tabby: Please!

Nick *(after a moment)*: There you go, I finally made it to level fourteen! Wow! *(pause)*

Nick: What a bummer, it looks like the rain out there is never going to end. Anyway, do you know where Mum and Dad are driving us to?

Tabby: Sure, I've been reading all about it in this travel guide, while you were playing that stupid game. We're driving to Stirling Castle – ever heard of it?

Nick: Yes, I think we learned about Stirling Castle in history class. Isn't it the most important castle in Scotland?

Tabby: Yes, it is. It's one of the largest and most important castles of the country. Several Scottish kings and queens were crowned at Stirling Castle, for example Mary, Queen of Scots, in 1543. She also lived there with her family.

Nick: Was that the same queen as Mary Stuart?

Tabby: Yes, Mary, Queen of Scots, and Mary Stuart were the same person. Didn't you know that? Anyway, did you know that when Mary, Queen of Scots, was crowned she was still a baby?

Nick: No, really?

Tabby: Yes. That was because her father, King James V, died shortly after she was born.

Nick: Hmmm … interesting. What else does your travel guide tell us about Stirling Castle?

Tabby: Here … Did you know that many people claim to have seen ghosts at Stirling Castle?

Nick: Really? That sounds cool.

Tabby: Yes. Listen to this: Several ghosts have reportedly been seen at Stirling Castle. The one seen most often is the so-called Highland Ghost. He was seen by both staff and visitors, and he was wearing a traditional Scottish costume. Some tourists first thought he was a tour guide, but then they saw him turn around, walk away and vanish in front of their eyes!

Nick: Wow!

Tabby: And listen to this *(reading excitedly)*: The Green Lady is another famous ghost in Stirling Castle. The legend is that she was a servant girl to Mary, Queen of Scots. One night while the queen was sleeping, and the servant girl was with her, the curtains of the queen's bed caught fire from a candle. Although she was able to save the queen's life, the servant girl was badly injured and died. Ever since, from time to time, a ghost has been seen in the castle, wearing green clothes – the same colour as the servant girl's clothes. This is why the ghost is called the Green Lady. And there are still some more ghosts!

Nick: Aha. Well, Tabby, let's see if we can find some of them at the castle …

Tabby *(giving Nick a punch)*: Stop it, Nick, you're so dumb. I'm frightened by all of these stories already!

Aufgabe 1

a) Scotland
Hinweis: *Z. 17 f.*

b) the same person.
Hinweis: *Z. 23*

c) was still a baby.
Hinweis: *Z. 24 f.*

d) "Highland Ghost".
Hinweis: *Z. 35 f.*

e) was badly injured when saving the queen's life.
Hinweis: *Z. 42 ff.*

f) clothes.
Hinweis: *Z. 45 f.*

Part 2

Tour guide: And now I would like to welcome you to the palace of Stirling Castle. It is one of the most remarkable Renaissance buildings in Britain. The palace was built in 1540 for King James V. The Scottish kings and queens used this palace as a royal residence until 1603. In 1603, King James VI also became King of England, and the royal court moved to London.
A few years ago, the palace of Stirling Castle was completely renovated for 12 million pounds. Artists from many countries made the interior look like it could have been in the 16th century, when Mary, Queen of Scots, was running around in the palace as a young girl. So the paintings and pieces of furniture you see in this hall are not the originals from the 16th century. This is why they have such a beautiful, fresh colour. *(fading)*

Nick *(whispers)*: Wow, Tabby, this is the greatest castle I've ever seen!

Tabby *(whispers back)*: Haven't I told you?

Nick: Yeah …

Tour guide *(fading in)*: In the castle you can also meet costumed characters, who demonstrate to the visitors what life in the palace and at the royal court was like in the 16th century. As you walk through the rooms, you will see servants, musicians, ambassadors and all sorts of characters.

Nick *(whispers)*: Cool, let's have a look and find some of these costumed characters.

Tabby *(whispers back)*: Yes, let's try!

Aufgabe 2

a) in 1540
Hinweis: *Z. 3 f.*

b) in 1603
Hinweis: *Z. 4 ff.*

c) to London
Hinweis: *Z. 5 f.*

d) 12 million pounds
Hinweis: *Z. 7 f.*

e) artists (from many countries)
Hinweis: *Z. 8 f.*

f) (the) 16th century
Hinweis: *Z. 16 ff.*

Part 3

Nick: Here, Tabby, let's stand under this archway. It's really too bad we left the umbrella inside the car!

Tabby: I wonder where Mum and Dad are now. I hope they aren't looking for us … Gosh, I'm all wet and cold!

Nick: I think they're still inside the palace, or in the souvenir shop. It's a pretty long tour, don't you think?

Tabby: Good for them, so they're at least inside! I told you we shouldn't have left the tour.

Nick: Let's go inside here for a moment. It's drier in there.

Tabby: Yes, it is.

Nick: Tabby, look!

Tabby: What?

Nick: There is another one of those costumed characters from the palace, over there in the shadow … She looks like a servant.

Tabby: What? Where? I can't see anyone.

Nick: Right there! Don't you see her? She's carrying something …

Tabby: *Where?* I don't see her!

Nick *(screams)*: Ahh!

Tabby: Nick, what happened? Did you step on something?

Nick: T … T … Tabby, you won't believe what I just saw!

Tabby *(frightened)*: What? What did you see?

Nick: T … T … The servant girl! Sh … Sh … She was standing there just a moment ago. She was carrying a basket or something. But then she just turned around and walked right into that wall.

Tabby *(screams)*: Ahh! What? Are you serious?

Nick: Yes! I … I … saw her … She was wearing a green dress and a white apron …

Tabby: Oh my God! Let's get out of here!

Nick: Right, let's leave this place!

Tabby: Oh my God! This is scary!!!

Aufgabe 3

0	1	2	3	4
A	C	D	G	I

Part 4

(In the car)

Tabby: You are such an idiot! I'll never tell you anything about any place we visit, ever again.

Nick: *(laughing)*

Tabby: You idiot!

Nick *(laughing)*: Sorry, it was just so funny ... you should have seen your face. The moment I told you the costumed servant disappeared into the wall ...

Tabby: Stop it! I hate you!

Nick: *(laughing)*

Tabby: For a moment I really believed you and thought there was a ghost!

Nick: *(laughing)* That was funny, wasn't it?

Tabby: Don't ever, ever do that again!

Nick: OK, I won't.

Tabby: Promise?

Nick: Sure, I promise. *(cracks up again and continues to laugh)*

Tabby: Ahh! I don't believe you! I swear I will NEVER go into ANY castle with you again!

Aufgabe 4

a) *wrong:* idiom, *correct:* idiot

b) *wrong:* teach, *correct:* tell

c) *wrong:* not, *correct:* just

d) *wrong:* trusted, *correct:* believed

e) *wrong:* palace, *correct:* castle

Übungsaufgaben
Lösungen zum „Sprachgebrauch"

Aufgabe 1

Beispiellösungen:

a) At school you find chalk, a blackboard and pupils, for example.

b) When it is cold in winter there is snow and ice.

c) In the zoo there are a lot of animals, for example monkeys, tigers and bears.

Aufgabe 2

Beispiellösungen:

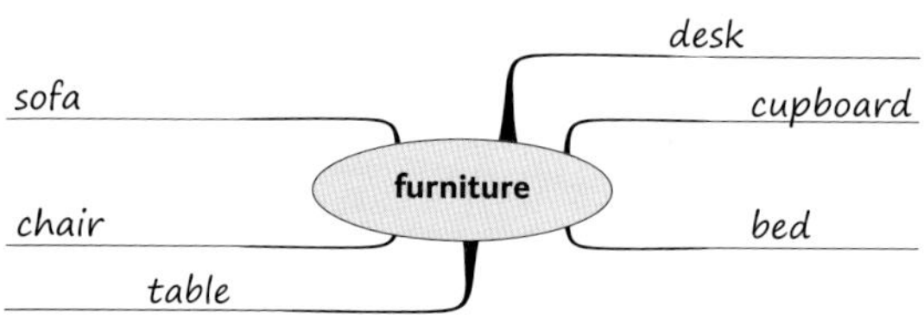

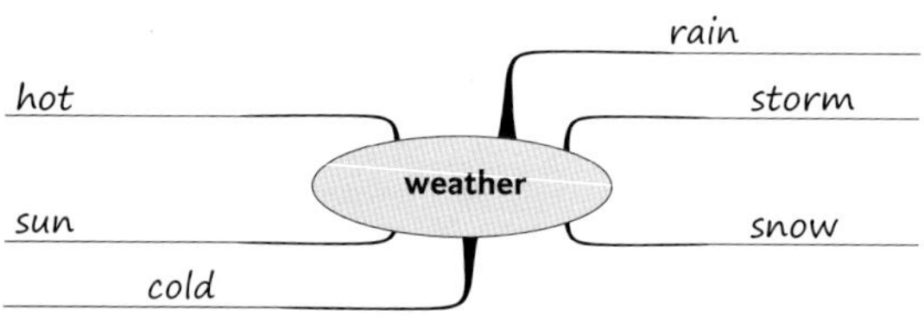

Aufgabe 3

Hinweis: *In dieser Aufgabe ist der Oberbegriff nicht vorgegeben. Du musst überlegen, was die aufgelisteten Wörter bzw. die Bilder gemeinsam haben.*

a) colours/colors

b) vehicles

c) languages

Aufgabe 4

Hinweis: *Zu Beginn jeder Zeile ist der Oberbegriff vorgegeben. Du musst also nur noch überlegen, welches Wort nicht dazu passt.*

a) pineapple
Hinweis: *kein Gemüse*

b) horse
Hinweis: *kein Fahrzeug*

c) vinegar
Hinweis: *kein Getränk*

d) fork
Hinweis: *keine Mahlzeit*

e) soft
Hinweis: *keine Geschmacksrichtung*

Aufgabe 5

Hinweis: *Hier musst du überlegen, welches Wort nicht in die Reihe passt, und was die verbliebenen Wörter gemeinsam haben.*

a) ~~bag~~ → clothes
Hinweis: *„bag" ist kein Kleidungsstück*

b) ~~pen~~ → car/bus/van/vehicles
Hinweis: *„pen" ist kein Teil eines Fahrzeugs*

c) ~~food~~ → parts of the body
Hinweis: *„food" ist kein Körperteil*

d) ~~knife~~ → vegetables
Hinweis: *„knife" ist kein Gemüse*

e) ~~meat~~ → desserts
Hinweis: *„meat" ist kein Nachtisch*

Aufgabe 6

a) restaurant
b) theatre
c) hospital
d) church
e) park

Aufgabe 7

board – bored
whole – hole
no – know
break – brake
hour – our
piece – peace
see – sea

Aufgabe 8

a) It was dark at • <u>in</u> • over the morning when I went to school.

b) The plane was left • <u>late</u> • soon this morning.

c) I often drive • <u>go</u> • miss by train.

d) What • Which • <u>Where</u> can I buy a watch, please?

Aufgabe 9

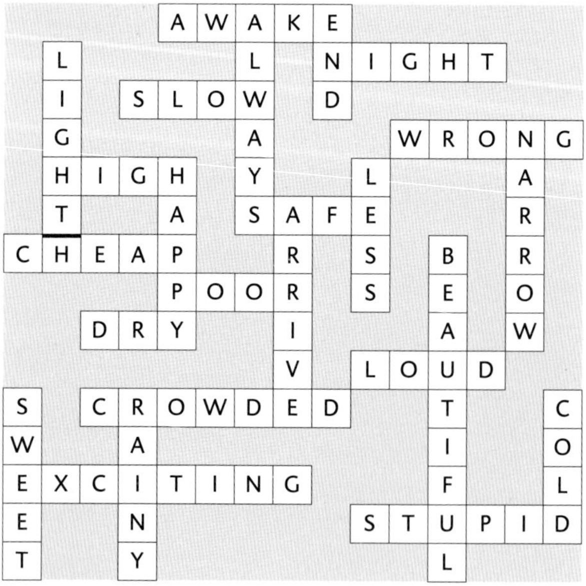

Aufgabe 10

Hinweis: *Im Englischen haben nur wenige Nomen eine eigene „weibliche" Form. Oft wird das Nomen (z. B. „teacher" = „Lehrer"/„Lehrerin") durch ein Pronomen (z. B. „he"/„his" oder „she"/„her") oder eine Ergänzung (z. B. „Mrs/Ms", „Mr") näher bestimmt, sodass klar ist, ob es sich um eine weibliche oder männliche Person handelt.*

a) policewoman
b) princess
c) actress
d) waitress

Aufgabe 11

a) knives
b) mice
c) men
d) women
e) children
f) fish
g) leaves
h) teeth

Aufgabe 12

a) railway station
b) travel agency
c) suitcase
d) passport

Aufgabe 13

a) a radio
b) a pen
c) a mobile phone
d) a key

Aufgabe 14

a) Big Ben is a tourist **a**ttraction in London.

b) The “Anne Frank House” is in Amsterdam. That is in the Netherlands. The people there are called the **D**utch.

c) The Leaning Tower of Pisa is in Italy. The people there **sp**eak Italian.

d) The Eiffel Tower is in Paris. Paris is the **c**apital of France.

e) The Puerta del Sol is in Madrid, in Spain. People from Spain are called **Sp**anish.

Aufgabe 15

Hinweis: *Hier musst du folgende Veränderungen vornehmen: „build“ (Verb) → „building“ (Nomen), „surprise“ (Nomen) → „surprisingly“ (Adverb), „beauty” (Nomen) → “beautiful” (Adjektiv), „sadness“ (Nomen) → „sad“ (Adjektiv nach Verben der Sinneswahrnehmung), „friendly“ (Adjektiv) → „friend“ (Nomen), „movement“ (Nomen) → move (Verb), „French“ (Adjektiv) → „France“ (Nomen)*

a) Where is the cafeteria? – It’s in the main **building**.

b) Do you like the food there? – Yes, it’s **surprisingly** good.

c) Who is that **beautiful** girl over there? – That’s my sister.

d) Why is she looking so **sad**? – Her **friend** Lili just moved away.

e) Where did she **move**? – Back to **France**.

Aufgabe 16

Hinweis: *Zur Kontrolle, ob du die Lücken korrekt ausgefüllt hast, lies dir am Ende den gesamten Text noch einmal durch. Wenn du merkst, dass manche Sätze keinen Sinn ergeben, musst du dir andere Lösungsmöglichkeiten überlegen.*

a) **Clara:** Hi Eric, how are you?

b) **Eric:** Fine, thanks. How are you?

c) **Clara:** I’m fine, too. But I miss you all.

d) **Eric:** We miss you, too. When are you coming home?

e) **Clara:** On Friday.

f) **Eric:** We’re looking forward to seeing you.

Aufgabe 17

Hinweis: *Hier musst du nicht auf die Verwendung der richtigen Zeit achten, da alle Verben in der Grundform (Infinitiv) eingesetzt werden.*

"I'm going to wear my suit and I think I will be very nervous. I hope I won't forget my lines. Even my grandparents want to come and see me acting. I hope everyone will enjoy the evening."

Aufgabe 18

Sara: "Lisa and I are going to Paris on 12th May."
Pierre: "When will you arrive in Paris?"
Sara: "At 2.35 pm."
Pierre: "What is the name of the hotel you're staying at?"
Sara: "It's Hôtel de Paris."
Pierre: "Do you have any plans for your stay?"
Sara: "I want to do some shopping/sightseeing and visit the Eiffel Tower and the Champs-Elysées."
Pierre: "I would like to show you the nightlife in Paris. I'm looking forward to seeing you next week."

Aufgabe 19

Hinweis: *Für die Verwendung der Präpositionen gibt es keine festen Regeln. Am besten lernst du die jeweiligen Präpositionen immer zusammen mit den entsprechenden Verben. In der Kurzgrammatik findest du eine Übersicht zu häufigen Präpositionen im Englischen.*

a) The teacher is sitting at the table.
b) Jessica has never been to Australia.
c) What do you think of my new dress?
d) The new boy in our class is from Singapore.
e) I am waiting for you at the bus stop.

Aufgabe 20

Hinweis: *Das Present progressive findest du in der Kurzgrammatik im Kapitel „Zeiten – tenses".*

a) What are you doing in this picture?

b) I am carrying a large watermelon I bought at the market.

c) The dress I am wearing in this picture is new.

d) The sun is shining in every picture.

e) Here we are going down to the beach.

Aufgabe 21

Hinweis: *Die Regeln zur Verwendung des Going-to-future kannst du in der Kurzgrammatik unter „Zeiten –* tenses*" nachlesen.*

a) I am going to meet Jane on Saturday for breakfast.

b) On Monday I am going to see the doctor.

c) I am going to go camping with some of my friends.

Aufgabe 22

Hinweis: *Das Simple past findest du in der Kurzgrammatik unter „Zeiten –* tenses*".*

On Saturday morning Kelly and Sara met in town to do some shopping. They were invited to a birthday party in the evening and wanted to buy a present. At first they couldn't really decide what to buy, but then they saw a cool smartphone case and were sure that that would be the right present for Tim. Now they could take a look around for some trendy clothes for the party. Kelly bought a T-shirt, but Sara didn't find anything. Afterwards they went home to get changed for the party.

Aufgabe 23

Hinweis: *Hier musst du entscheiden, welche Zeitform korrekt ist. Signalwörter, z. B. „yesterday", „now" „last week", helfen dir dabei, die richtige Zeit anzuwenden. Du kannst dazu noch einmal alle Regeln in der Kurzgrammatik nachlesen.*

a) I felt very sick yesterday, so I went to bed early and now I'm feeling/I feel much better.

b) In 1982, my brother was born.

c) I am going to move/I am moving to Australia in October. I can't stand the English weather any longer.

d) My aunt gave me this book for my birthday last week.

Aufgabe 24

a) Do you have tickets for the Rihanna concert?
b) No, I'm sorry. We sold the last one yesterday.
c) What a pity! But what about the open air festival which takes place in August?
d) Yes, we still have tickets for the festival.

Aufgabe 25

1	2	3	4
C	A	D	B

Aufgabe 26

Hinweis: *Adverbien beschreiben u. a., auf welche Art und Weise etwas geschieht.*

a) gladly
b) easily
c) well
d) closely

Aufgabe 27

Hinweis: *Die Signalwörter für die Verwendung des Simple present findest du in der Kurzgrammatik unter „Zeiten –* tenses*". Beachte bei der Bildung des Simple present den Merksatz: „He, she, it – ‚s' muss mit!"*

a) Mum always **wakes** me up in the morning.
b) Sally often **goes** hiking at the weekends.
c) Every year, Mr Jones **spends** his holidays in Ireland.
d) On Mondays, Jane **is** always late for school. The rest of the week she usually **arrives** on time.
e) Lisa never **does** her homework properly.

Aufgabe 28

Hinweis: *Die Regeln zur Steigerung von Adjektiven findest du in der Kurzgrammatik unter „Steigerung und Vergleich –* comparisons*".*

a) Jessica is taller than Jenny.

b) Jim is the tallest boy in our class.

c) Sara has the longest/(long) hair.

d) Michelle's hair is darker than Tina's.

e) Toby is better at playing football than Mark.

f) But Lisa is the best player!

Aufgabe 29

Hinweis: *Entscheide auch hier, ob du die 1. oder die 2. Steigerungsform einsetzen musst. Hinzu kommt auch der Vergleich mit „as ... as".*

Danny:
The weather in France was much worse than last year. It was raining almost all the time. Our flat, however, was more comfortable than last year. I also like the French food. It's much better than the food in England. In my opinion, France is the most beautiful country in Europe.

Luisa:
I went to Spain with a youth group. The weather in San Sebastian was almost as bad as in France, but it was more exciting to spend the holidays there than with my parents in Scotland. In my opinion, Spanish food is the best in Europe. My holiday in Spain was great, and I met more people than in all my holidays before!

Aufgabe 30

Hinweis: *Hier musst du die fehlenden Pronomen (Fürwörter) einsetzen. Die Regeln zur Verwendung von Pronomen findest du in der Kurzgrammatik.*

Mrs Brown comes into the classroom, looks out of the window and asks her class in surprise, "Whose jacket is that lying outside?" John answers, "It is Lisa's." "Lisa, is that true? Is that your jacket?" Mrs Brown asks. "Go and get it, please." Then Mrs Brown notices that Lisa is not in the classroom. "Where is she today?" "I think she is ill," says Maggie, who sounds as if she has been crying, "She didn't wait for me this morning like she usually does. I borrowed her jacket yesterday and she told me to look after it. But this morning, Jack and Tim took the jacket and threw it around. I couldn't catch it, and then they threw it out of the window." "Is that true, you two?" asks Mrs Brown, "Did you do that? Go and get the jacket immediately, give it back to Maggie and say sorry to her. You will stay behind after school and clean up the classroom." Jack is very angry and says, "It wasn't me!" He points at Tim: "He did it – it was all his fault!" Mrs Brown turns to the whole class and says, "All of you saw them take the jacket and throw it out of the window, and did any of you help Maggie? No, you didn't. I have decided that you will all stay behind after school and clean up the classroom. Maggie, you go to Lisa's house straight after school, return the jacket to her and explain what we/ they did at school today. And now, everyone, please show me your homework!"

Aufgabe 31

Hinweis: *Die Regeln zu den Relativsätzen und zur Verwendung der Relativpronomen kannst du in der Kurzgrammatik nachlesen.*

a) Doesn't the pullover which is lying on the floor belong to you?

b) The man who lives next door had an accident yesterday.

c) The book which you lent me last week was really exciting.

d) The woman who is sitting next to you is my mother.

e) The train which arrived late was very crowded.

Aufgabe 32

Hinweis: *Die Regeln zu den* if-clauses *kannst du in der Kurzgrammatik unter „Bedingungssätze –* if-clauses*" nachlesen.*

a) If I take the train, I will be late.

b) If you don't take an umbrella with you, you will get wet.

c) If I move to America, I will improve my English.

d) I won't tell you, even if you ask me a hundred times.

Aufgabe 33

a) I would like a loaf of bread, please.

b) Could you tell me the way to the next bus station?

c) I'd like to have the menu, please.

d) Do you have this pair of jeans one size bigger?

Aufgabe 34

Hinweis: *Die Regeln zur Wortstellung kannst du in der Kurzgrammatik unter „Wortstellung –* word order*" nachlesen.*

a) Paul is going to visit his aunt and uncle in California.

b) They invited him to spend the summer with them.

c) Zoe is jealous that her brother is going to make a trip.

d) Zoe's aunt promises that she can visit them soon, too.

Aufgabe 35

a) Where are you from?/Where do you live?

b) How old are you?

c) Why are you here?

d) Do you like it here?/Do you like this town?

e) Have you ever been here before?

Aufgabe 36

Hinweis: *Die Regeln zur Bildung der Verneinung findest du unter „Zeiten –* tenses*"*

a) The sun isn't shining outside.

b) Mr Weaver didn't enjoy the film he watched yesterday.

c) The Smiths don't have/haven't got a new car.

d) Sara doesn't have/hasn't got a dog.

e) The weather forecast says it won't rain tomorrow.

f) The Millers aren't travelling around Europe.

Aufgabe 37

Hinweis: *Lies zuerst den ganzen Text und versuche, den Inhalt trotz der Lücken zu erschließen. Konzentriere dich dann auf jeden einzelnen Satz. Dabei kann es hilfreich sein, die Sätze in deine Muttersprache zu übersetzen. Wenn dir das fehlende Wort eingefallen ist, überprüfe es noch einmal im Satzzusammenhang. So erkennst du, ob das Wort auch die richtige grammatikalische Form (z. B. Zeitform) hat.*

(1) ask questions = Fragen stellen; Signalwort „yesterday" → asked (Simple past)
(2) ask questions about = Fragen stellen über/zu

(3) subject = Unterrichtsfach
(4) there is = es gibt
(5) Relativpronomen „which/that" (welches, das) → bezieht sich auf das Football-Team; „who" kann sich nur auf Personen beziehen; oder: Konjunktion „and"
(6) how = wie
(7) be quite OK = ziemlich in Ordnung sein

Hi Brian,

Yesterday I met my tutor, Mr Castiello, (0) **at** school. He (1) **asked** me a lot of questions, for example (2) **about** my family or what it was like at my old school. He already knew that Maths is my favourite (3) **subject**, so I'm going to be in an honors class again. The good news: (4) **There** is a football team at the new school (5) **which/that/and** I can join right away. The next practice is already tomorrow afternoon. This is great! Let's see (6) **how** good this team is and what matches they have with other schools. Thinking about it, my new school could actually (7) **be** quite OK!

Take care,
Jason

Aufgabe 38

Hinweis: *Lies erst den ganzen Text durch, um einen Eindruck zu gewinnen, wovon er handelt. Sollten dir hier schon Fehler auffallen, markiere sie. Gehe den Text dann Satz für Satz durch – die Fehler befinden sich übrigens immer in den Zeilen neben den Linien, auf die du das richtige Wort schreibst. Um das korrekte Wort zu finden, kann es hilfreich sein, die Sätze in deine Muttersprache zu übersetzen. Im Folgenden sind die richtigen Lösungen fett gedruckt.*

0. *my = besitzanzeigendes Fürwort „mein"*
1. *in the middle of sth. = feststehender Ausdruck („mitten im Schuljahr")*
2. *Mrs Stephenson → she*
3. *22 students = Mehrzahl → are*
4. *girls and boys = zählbare Namenwörter → many*
5. *Justin (= he) → lives (3. Person Singular: „he, she, it: -s muss mit")*
6. *will/are going to (Formen, die etwas Zukünftiges ausdrücken), can/could (modale Hilfsverben) → können hier mit „be" kombiniert werden*

Dear diary,
Today was **0. my** (~~me~~) first day at the new school. It was OK. I was a bit nervous because I am joining a new class in the middle **1. of** (~~for~~) the year. All of the other

students already know each other and I am the only new kid. But my new teacher, Mrs Stephenson, was really nice and **2. she** (~~he~~) introduced me to the whole class. There **3. are** (~~is~~) 22 students in the class, just about as **4. many** (~~much~~) girls as boys. I sit next to Justin, who also **5. lives** (~~live~~) in my neighborhood. Let's see, maybe we **6. will/are going to/can/could** (~~were~~) be friends.

Übungsaufgaben
Lösungen zum „Leseverstehen"

Allgemeiner Hinweis: *In diesem Kapitel kannst du das Leseverstehen trainieren. Hier werden neben Fragen zum groben Verständnis auch Details abgefragt. Lies den Text deshalb besonders aufmerksam und nimm ihn immer wieder zur Hand, während du die zugehörigen Aufgaben bearbeitest. Verwende bei sprachlichen Unklarheiten auch das Wörterbuch.*

TEST 1: Treasure hunting at the Florida Keys

Vokabelhinweise:
Z. 2 f.: treasure hunter: Schatzjäger
Z. 10: dedication: Hingabe
Z. 30: goods: hier: Frachtgut, Waren
Z. 37: to remain: bleiben
Z. 39: to accompany: begleiten
Z. 41 f.: daughter-in-law: Schwiegertochter
Z. 59: cargo: Fracht
Z. 63: emerald: Smaragd (ein Edelstein)
Z. 63: artefacts: Artefakte – hier: von Menschen hergestellte Gegenstände
Z. 83: to be convinced: überzeugt sein

Aufgabe 1

Hinweis: *Finde zu jedem Abschnitt die passende Überschrift. Eine Auswahl an Überschriften (A–G) ist vorgegeben. Wenn du die einzelnen Textabschnitte sorgfältig durchliest, wird es dir leichtfallen, die jeweils inhaltlich passende Überschrift zu finden.*

paragraph ❶ (lines 1–12)	C
paragraph ❷ (lines 13–27)	G
paragraph ❸ (lines 28–48)	E
paragraph ❹ (lines 49–68)	D
paragraph ❺ (lines 69–80)	A
paragraph ❻ (lines 81–90)	F

Aufgabe 2

	T	F	N
a) The *Atocha* was a Spanish ship.	✓		
b) Mel Fisher and his wife Dolores had a surf shop in California.		✓	
c) Mel and Dolores married in 1953.			✓
d) The *Atocha* was on her way to Havanna when she sank.		✓	
e) The treasure is worth about 40 million dollars.		✓	
f) You can also go on diving tours to the shipwreck site.	✓		

Zu c): **Hinweis:** *Zwar haben Mel und Dolores im Jahr 1953 geheiratet, aber diese Information steht nicht im Text.*

Aufgabe 3

Hinweis: *In der Aufgabe sind verschiedene Jahreszahlen angegeben. Finde im Text das Ereignis, das im jeweiligen Jahr stattfand.*

❶	❷	❸	❹	❺	❻	❼
H	B	F	D	G	C	E

Aufgabe 4

Hinweis: *Beantworte die Fragen anhand der Informationen aus dem Text. Es reicht, wenn du in Stichworten oder kurzen Sätzen antwortest.*

a) He had a "dive shop" and gave scuba diving trainings.
Hinweis: *Z. 16 ff.*

b) 5/five
Hinweis: *Z. 35 f.*

c) a (Spanish) ship/a sister ship of the *Atocha*
Hinweis: *Z. 46 f.*

d) to make sure the treasures were collected properly/not damaged
Hinweis: *Z. 65 ff.*

e) navigational instruments, military equipment, objects of native American origin, tools, ceramics, seeds, insects
Hinweis: *Z. 75 ff.*

Vokabelhinweise:
Z. 3: annual: jährlich
Z. 5: scenery: Landschaft
Z. 6: cameleer: Kameltreiber/in
Z. 8: bet: Wette
Z. 14: to provide: (zur Verfügung) stellen
Z. 48 f.: Overland Telegraph Line: Telegrafenleitung, die durch ganz Australien gelegt wurde
Z. 49 f.: water supply infrastructure: Wasserversorgungsnetz
Z. 58: plant species: Pflanzenarten
Z. 58 f.: to pollute: verschmutzen
Z. 72: breeding: Zucht

Aufgabe 1

a) Australia
Hinweis: *Z. 3*

b) camel race.
Hinweis: *Z. 6 f.*

c) made a bet with a friend.
Hinweis: *Z. 8 ff.*

d) Australia.
Hinweis: *Z. 20 ff.*

e) they can transport goods and are used to the heat.
Hinweis: *Z. 27 ff.*

f) Australians spend a lot of money.
Hinweis: *Z. 61 ff.*

Aufgabe 2

Hinweis: *Im Lesetext fehlen verschiedene Sätze. Wähle für jede Lücke den passenden Satz aus und notiere den jeweiligen Buchstaben (A–G) in der Tabelle. Beachte, dass ein Satz in keine Lücke passt.*

❶	❷	❸	❹	❺	❻
E	D	A	G	C	F

Aufgabe 3

Hinweis: *Die Aufgabe enthält mehrere Aussagen, die alle sinngemäß im Lesetext zu finden sind. Suche nun die Stellen im Text, an denen diese Information vorkommen und gib die entsprechenden Zeilen an.*

a) lines 10–12
b) lines 29/30
c) lines 32–34
d) lines 71/72

Aufgabe 4

Hinweis: *Hier reicht es, wenn du die Fragen mit kurzen Sätzen oder Stichworten beantwortest, die du dem Text entnehmen kannst.*

a) up to 40 km
 Hinweis: *Z. 30 f.*
b) He was injured by his camel and died (because of the wounds).
 Hinweis: *Z. 39 ff.*
c) too many camels/eat 80 % of plant species/pollute water holes/damage water systems/they were set free
 Hinweis: *Z. 53 ff.*
d) export of live camels/export of camel meat/camel milk products
 Hinweis: *Z. 66 ff.*

TEST 3: Is autonomous driving becoming a reality?

Vokabelhinweise:
Z. 3: autonomous: eigenständig
Z. 7: driving license: Führerschein
Z. 9: to fail: versagen, ausfallen
Z. 11 f.: to be made responsible: verantwortlich gemacht werden
Z. 15 f.: intention: Absicht, Zweck
Z. 17: to increase: erhöhen
Z. 19: to request: hier: verlangen
Z. 20: measures: Maßnahmen
Z. 29: to improve: verbessern
Z. 31: to avoid: vermeiden
Z. 40: lane: Spur
Z. 41: blind spot: „toter Winkel“

Z. 65: loss: Verlust
Z. 68: to blame sb: jmd. die Schuld geben
Z. 69: car manufacturer: Autohersteller
Z. 72: regulations: Vorschriften, Bestimmungen
Z. 81: to announce: ankündigen
Z. 89: to estimate: schätzen

Aufgabe 1

Hinweis: *Ordne den Textabschnitten die richtige Überschrift zu. Beachte, dass drei Überschriften nicht passen und somit nicht zugeordnet werden können.*

paragraph B	paragraph C	paragraph D	paragraph E	paragraph F
7	4	6	1	3

Aufgabe 2

Hinweis: *Notiere die Aussagen, die mit den Informationen des Lesetextes übereinstimmen.*

1. b
2. d
3. e
4. g
5. j

Aufgabe 3

Hinweis: *Hier sind Aussagen aufgelistet, die inhaltlich alle im Text vorkommen, jedoch etwas anders formuliert sind als im Text selbst. Suche die entsprechenden Textstellen heraus und notiere, in welche(n) Zeile(n) diese stehen.*

❶	❷	❸	❹	❺
line(s) 19–22	line(s) 38–40	line(s) 50–52	line(s) 63–65	line(s) 77–80

Aufgabe 4

Hinweis: *Hier sind Wörter vorgegeben, die im Text vorkommen. Diese Wörter können unterschiedliche Bedeutungen haben. Lies auf S. 31 jedes Wort im Satzzusammenhang und finde heraus, welche deutsche Entsprechung jeweils Sinn ergibt.*

b) Fall c) wichtigste/wesentliche d) warnen e) Führung

Vokabelhinweise:
Z. 14: to contribute: beitragen
Z. 21 f.: U-21 development squad: hier: Mannschaft für unter 21-Jährige, die weiter aufgebaut werden sollen
Z. 46 f.: Confederation of African Football: Afrikanischer Fußballbund
Z. 50 f.: to suggest: hier: nahelegen, andeuten
Z. 52: to aspire: anstreben
Z. 55: devotion: Hingabe
Z. 55: obstacle: Hindernis
Z. 75: to make an effort: sich anstrengen, sich bemühen
Z. 76: deceased: verstorben
Z. 83 f.: to support: unterstützen
Z. 84: confidence: Zuversicht
Z. 87: to achieve: erreichen
Z. 89: to focus on sth: sich auf etwas konzentrieren

Aufgabe 1

Hinweis: *Entscheide, ob die Aussagen richtig (True/T) oder falsch (False/F) sind bzw. ob es dazu im Text keine Informationen gibt (Not in the text/N).*

	T	F	N
a) Kelechi plays for the national football team of Nigeria and played for the first team of Manchester City.	✓		
b) Kelechi never had any doubts that he would make it to the top.		✓	
c) Besides a Nigerian passport, Kelechi also has a British passport. **Hinweis:** *Es wird nicht erwähnt, welchen Pass Kelechi hat.*			✓
d) Kelechi still has family in Nigeria.	✓		
e) It was Kelechi's dream to become team captain of Manchester City one day.			✓
f) Kelechi lives together with his father.		✓	

Aufgabe 2

Hinweis: *Bringe die Fakten in die zeitlich richtige Reihenfolge. Der überzählige Satz passt inhaltlich nicht zum Lesetext.*

1. e
   Hinweis: *Z. 56 ff.*

2. d
   Hinweis: *Z. 34 f.*
3. f
   Hinweis: *Z. 20 ff.*
4. c
   Hinweis: *Z. 17 ff.*

Aufgabe 3

Hinweis: *Beantworte die Fragen auf Grundlage des Lesetextes. Schreibe keine langen Sätze aus dem Text ab, sondern beschränke dich auf kurze (Teil-)Sätze bzw. Stichpunkte.*

a) (in) Nigeria
   Hinweis: *33 ff.*

b) Most Promising Talent of the Year
   Hinweis: *45 f.*

c) 18 (years old)
   Hinweis: *47 ff.*

d) 3/three (two brothers and one sister)
   Hinweis: *72 ff.*

e) to be/become a great player
   Hinweis: *91 f.*

Aufgabe 4

Hinweis: *Finde die Stellen im Lesetext, die inhaltlich mit den Aussagen übereinstimmen. Notiere anschließend die Fundstellen durch Angabe der jeweiligen Zeilen.*

a) lines 30–32
b) lines 51–53
c) lines 66–69
d) lines 83/84
e) lines 92/93

Übungsaufgaben
Lösungen zur „Sprachmittlung“

Allgemeiner Hinweis: *In diesem Kapitel geht es um die Sprachmittlung vom Englischen ins Deutsche. Dabei musst du nicht Wort für Wort übersetzen – es reicht, wenn du die wesentliche Aussage eines Textes wiedergibst.*

TEST 1: Signs and posters

Aufgabe 1

a) Wir müssen hier auf dem Weg bleiben. / Wir dürfen den Weg nicht verlassen.

b) Die Straße ist wegen Überflutung gesperrt.

c) Man soll die Füchse und alle anderen Tiere im Park nicht füttern. (Die Wildtiere sollen auch wild bleiben.)

Hinweis: *Den Zusatz in Klammern musst du nicht unbedingt erwähnen. Im Mittelpunkt steht die Information, dass die Tiere nicht gefüttert werden sollen.*

d) Das hier ist ein Rastplatz – außerdem kommt in zwei Meilen eine Touristeninformation.

e) Im Park darf man nicht übernachten oder campen.

Hinweis: *„Sleeping“ kann man hier etwas freier mit „übernachten“ übersetzen.*

Aufgabe 2

Hinweis: *Die folgenden Lösungen sind Beispiele. Achte jedoch darauf, genau auf die Fragen einzugehen. Formuliere deine Antworten so, wie du dich auch in einer echten Gesprächssituation ausdrücken würdest.*

a) Ja, das ist ein Herbstfest.

b) Das Fest findet morgen/diesen Samstag, also am 15. Oktober, statt. Es beginnt um 8 Uhr abends.

c) Es gibt Musik und Spiele, und man kann auch Preise gewinnen.

d) Nein, der Eintritt ist frei.

Aufgabe 3

a) Es gibt ein (komplettes) englisches Frühstück für 3,95 £, inklusive Kaffee oder Tee, oder ein großes Brötchen mit einer Wurst oder (Schinken)speck für 2,99 £. Dazu gibt es ebenfalls Tee oder Kaffee.

b) Nein, es gibt noch mehr. Man kann nach der vollständigen Frühstückskarte fragen.
Hinweis: *„Full breakfast menu" = vollständige Frühstückskarte; diese ist erhältlich („available"), d. h. man kann danach fragen.*

c) Frühstück gibt es (täglich) bis 11.30 Uhr.

d) Ja, man kann das Frühstück auch mitnehmen.

TEST 2: Wimbledon

Ball girls/boys: Die Ballmädchen und -jungen helfen bei den Spielen. Sie sind im Durchschnitt 15 Jahre alt und kommen aus Schulen in der Umgebung (von Wimbledon).

Strawberries: Traditionell werden in Wimbledon Erdbeeren mit Sahne gegessen – jedes Jahr sind das um die zwei Millionen Erdbeeren und 7 000 Liter Sahne.

Centre Court: Der Centre Court ist der wichtigste Tennisplatz in Wimbledon und befindet sich deshalb in der Mitte. Dort haben 15 000 Leute Platz. Hier befindet sich auch die *Royal Box*, die für die königliche Familie und andere VIPs reserviert ist.

Tickets: Um ein Ticket zu bekommen, kann man entweder an einer Verlosung teilnehmen oder man stellt sich die Nacht über an, um eine Karte für das Spiel am nächsten Tag zu bekommen.

TEST 3: Bungee jumping rules

Hinweis: *In der folgenden Beispiellösung sind für dich zur Orientierung zusätzlich noch jeweils in Klammern die Punkte angegeben, auf die du laut Aufgabenstellung eingehen musst.*

Liebe Tante Emina,

du überlegst doch schon seit einiger Zeit, einen Bungee-Sprung zu machen. Ich habe hier ein paar interessante Informationen darüber gefunden:
(Ausrüstung:) Fürs Bungeespringen brauchst du folgende Ausrüstung: Wanderschuhe, dicke Kleidung und einen Helm.

(Verbote:) Beachte, dass man nicht springen darf, wenn man ein gesundheitliches Problem hat (Herzprobleme, Bluthochdruck, Rückenprobleme), schwanger ist oder Alkohol getrunken hat.
(Vorgehen nach dem Sprung:) Nach dem Sprung wirst du vom Sprungseil abgehängt und mit einem Boot ans Flussufer gebracht.
(Zwei weitere Tipps:) Diese wichtigen Tipps habe ich noch für dich:

- Leere deine Taschen vor dem Sprung. /
- Nimm vor dem Sprung deine Brille ab. /
- Befolge immer die Anweisungen des Personals.
- Gehe mit einer positiven Einstellung in den Sprung. /
- Versuche während des Sprungs nicht zu schreien (wenn du cool sein willst).

Hoffentlich hilft dir das, eine Entscheidung zu treffen.

Viele Grüße,

Isabel

TEST 4: Undara Lava Tubes

Aufgabe 1

Du: Ich habe im Internet ein interessantes Ausflugsziel gefunden. Die „Undara Lava Tubes" im Undara-Vulkan-Nationalpark.
Dein Vater: Wie kann ich mir die Lava-Tunnel vorstellen?
Du: Wie ein Höhlensystem.
Dein Vater: Wie weit sind die „Lava Tubes" von Cairns entfernt?
Du: 275 Kilometer.
Dein Vater: Wann sind sie denn entstanden?
Du: Vor ungefähr 190 000 Jahren.
Dein Vater: „Undara" – hat dieser Name eigentlich eine besondere Bedeutung?
Du: Ja, er bedeutet „langer Weg" (– das ist ein Wort aus der Sprache der indigenen Bevölkerung Australiens).
Dein Vater: Seit wann können die Lava-Höhlen von Touristen besichtigt werden?
Du: Seit 1989 (gibt es geführte Touren).
Dein Vater: Ist es eine gute Idee, jetzt im August dort hinzufahren?
Du: Ja, weil es im August trocken ist.
Dein Vater: Ich überlege gerade, ob wir eine geführte Tour buchen sollten. Mit welchen Gefahren müssen wir rechnen, wenn wir die Lava-Tunnel allein erkunden?
Du: Man kann in verborgene Löcher stürzen und in manchen Höhlen kann man ersticken (wegen der hohen Konzentration an CO_2).

Dein Vater: Welche Übernachtungsmöglichkeiten gibt es in der Nähe der Lavahöhlen?

Du: **Ein Motel und einen Campingplatz (für Wohnwägen) in Mount Surprise oder restaurierte Eisenbahnwaggons, die über hundert Jahre alt sind.**

Aufgabe 2

Also, ich habe Folgendes herausgefunden ...

a) Touren finden um 8.00, 10.30 und 13.00 Uhr statt. Sie dauern jeweils zwei Stunden.

b) Auf der Tour besichtigt man drei Bereiche des Lavatunnel-Systems. Der Guide erzählt außerdem etwas zu Umweltaspekten, zur Geschichte und zu geologischen Merkmalen.

c) Die Tour ist körperlich nur wenig anstrengend.
(Ob eine Tour stattfindet, hängt auch vom Wetter ab.)
Die Tour ist nicht geeignet, wenn man einen Kinderwagen dabei hat, einen Rollstuhl oder eine Gehhilfe benötigt oder ansonsten in der Beweglichkeit eingeschränkt ist. (Man sollte die Tour auch vorab telefonisch reservieren.)

TEST 1: Bungee jumping in New Zealand

Bungee jumping in New Zealand

When you do a bungee jump you do this:
You jump from a great height, like a bridge, tower, platform or crane while you are safely connected to a cord.

Famous places to go bungee jumping in New Zealand:
bridge at the Kawaru River, Nevis bungee jumping platform (Greenhithe Bridge)

Famous sportsman who introduced bungee jumping as a business:
AJ Hackett

Most important safety device while bungee jumping:
body harness

Common reasons for fatal accidents during a jump:
cord is too long or jumpers become detached when using only an ankle attachment

TEST 2: Puppies

Details:

gender	*male*
quantity	three
breeding	mongrels (terrier, poodle + ??)
age	6 weeks
fur colour	grey (to black)
type of hair	straight
health care	checked by the vet / vaccinated
cost / price	for free
pick-up time	next month / once they're eight weeks old
recommendations	house-training / dog training

Hinweis: *Bei dieser Aufgabe sollst du auf Folgendes eingehen: Gib an, wo Deepa wohnt, was sie in Kovalam unternimmt, welche Sehenswürdigkeiten es dort gibt und wie das Strandleben dort aussieht.*

Beispiellösung:

Dear Mum and Dad,

I hope you're fine. I'm writing to tell you that I'm having such a great time here in Kovalam. Aunt Divya and Uncle Kumar are being really nice and they let me spend the days on my own. They also gave me a room all to myself.
There are a lot of tourists in Kovalam, but that's no surprise as the beach is beautiful and clean. There are a lot of Indian and western tourists and everyone is having a good time. I also went swimming and really enjoyed it!
Yesterday, I watched the fishermen bring in their traditional nets. I also went for a walk. I didn't go to any cafés because it would feel funny to go into a café without any friends, but I did make it up to the Vizhinjam lighthouse, which gives you a lovely view of the bay!

Love,
Deepa

Übungsaufgaben
Lösungen zum „Schreiben“

Allgemeiner Hinweis: *Für das gesamte Kapitel „Schreiben“ ist es wichtig, dass du dir die Arbeitsschritte zum Verfassen eines Textes im Trainingsband genau durchliest und dementsprechend arbeitest. Wenn du nach diesen Schritten vorgehst, wird dir ein gut strukturierter Text bestimmt nicht mehr schwerfallen. Die folgenden Lösungen sind Beispiele, an denen du dich orientieren kannst.*

Aufgabe 1

Hinweis: *Hier musst du noch keinen vollständigen Text schreiben, sondern einen vorgegebenen Satz abändern. Du kannst dabei üben, Sätze sprachlich zu variieren.*

a) I like **our house**, which **is old / is at the end of the street**.

b) At the end of **the street** you find **our (old) house**.

c) The street ends where **our (old) house is**.

d) Do you know the house **at the end of the street**? It's **our house/ours/old**.

e) Our **house** is **old** and **at the end of the street**.

Aufgabe 2

Hinweis: *Konjunktionen helfen dir, Sätze elegant zu verknüpfen und diese nicht nur aneinanderzureihen. Es ist hilfreich, wenn du sie mit Beispielsätzen in deine Vokabelkartei aufnimmst. Zu den deutschen Entsprechungen der englischen Konjunktionen vergleiche das entsprechende Kapitel in der Kurzgrammatik.*

a) **After / When** I left the house this morning I noticed that I had left behind my umbrella.

b) I would have needed it **because** it started to rain.

c) **As** I did not want to get wet I took the bus.

d) **When** I got off the bus, it was still raining.

e) It rained so heavily **that** I got completely wet.

f) **Although** I drank a cup of hot tea in the office, I was ill the next day **and** had to stay in bed.

Aufgabe 3

Hinweis: *Die Aufgabenstellung enthält ein Bild mit Stichwörtern, auf deren Grundlage du eine Geschichte schreiben sollst. Betrachte zuerst das Bild: zwei junge Leute trampen, der Zeitraum ist vorgegeben („Last August ..."). Überlege in einem zweiten Schritt, welchen (Reise-)plan die jungen Leute wohl haben. Welches unerwartete Ereignis könnte eintreten und wie fühlen sich die einzelnen Personen dabei? Im nächsten Schritt wählst du deine besten Ideen aus. Welche Ideen kannst du der Einleitung, dem Hauptteil und dem Schluss zuordnen? Verbinde deine Sätze mit Konjunktionen (z. B. „and", „because", „while"). Schreibe in der Zeitform „Simple past" (z. B. was/were, wanted ...). Verwende auch die wörtliche Rede, um deine Geschichte lebendiger zu machen.*

a) *Beispiellösung Notizen:*

Reiseziel, Pläne:
- hitchhike to a music festival in Italy
- not enough money for the trip: work and travel:
  Jessica: waitress in a café
  Jesse: plays the guitar in the pedestrian zone

Unerwartetes Ereignis, Gefühle:
- Jessica meets an Italian guy in the café
- Jesse is angry

b) *Beispiellösung Geschichte:*

Summer trip

Last August, Jessica and her older brother Jesse were on their way to a music festival in Italy. They did not have enough money to pay for the trip so they decided to hitchhike. They were lucky because some friendly drivers gave them a lift.

After arriving at the small Italian town at the coast Jessica soon found a job as a waitress at a café. Jesse played his guitar in the pedestrian zone, but he was not very successful. When the music festival started, a good-looking guest said to Jessica: "Hi, my name is Alberto. Would you like to go to the festival with me?" "What a cute guy!" thought Jessica. At the festival, Jessica and Alberto were flirting all the time, while Jesse was sitting next to them feeling alone and depressed. His sister was having a good time and he didn't even have enough money to buy himself a drink! "That is certainly not my idea of a great holiday!" Jesse thought angrily. *(166 words)*

Aufgabe 4

Hinweis: *Wie bei Aufgabe 4 wird dir ein Bild vorgegeben, bei dem zwei junge Leute per Anhalter unterwegs sind. Diesmal ist das Thema durch das Bild und die Vorgaben stärker eingegrenzt. Bei näherer Betrachtung der Zeichnung erfährst du zum einen, wohin die Fahrt gehen soll, nämlich nach Dublin, die Hauptstadt von Irland. Zum anderen trägt der junge Mann einen ausgefallenen Hut, der aufgrund seiner Form und des „Shamrocks" (Kleeblatt) auf die Feiern zum St. Patrick's Day hinweist. Die Wortvorgabe „Pleiten, Pech und Pannen" weist darauf hin, dass während des Trips das ein oder andere schiefgeht.*

Beispiellösung Notizen:

Anreise:
- Tina and Tom: hitchhiking to Dublin, it starts to rain
- bus stops: tour bus with musicians, singing and music during the trip

Pleiten, Pech und Pannen:
- forgot their backpack at the side of the road

Erlebnisse, Pleiten, Pech und Pannen:
- Dublin full of tourists, hotels fully booked
- train back home the same evening

Rückkehr:
- watch the St. Patrick's Day parade on TV the next day

Beispiellösung Geschichte:

A trip to remember

The day before St. Patrick's Day, Tina and Tom wanted to hitchhike to Dublin. While they were waiting at side of the road, it started to rain and they didn't have an umbrella with them. Unfortunately, no cars went past, but suddenly a bus stopped nearby. Inside was a cheerful band that was also going to Dublin to play in the parade the next day. "Welcome aboard!" said the band leader. After an hour of music and singing, they arrived in Dublin. That was when Tina and Tom realised that they had left their backpack at the side of the road, so Tina phoned home: "Mum, could you please get our backpack?" Her mother wasn't happy about that. Luckily, they had their money and valuables *(Wertsachen)* with them. In the next few hours they looked for a hotel room. "Sorry, we're fully booked" was what all the receptionists said. With no place to sleep, Tina and Tom decided to take the night train back home. The next day the two unlucky friends watched the St. Patrick's Day parade on TV. *(180 words)*

Aufgabe 5

Hinweis: *In den vorgegeben Bildern wird eine kurze Geschichte erzählt. Fasse sie in Worte und finde einen passenden und interessanten Schluss. Die Bildergeschichte lässt dir viel Raum für eigene Ideen, da das Ende offen ist. Du kannst folgendermaßen vorgehen:*
Schritt 1: Betrachtung der Bilder: ein junger Mann (Luke) geht im Park spazieren und schaut auf sein Handy, da er eine Textnachricht erhalten hat; vor seinen Füßen liegt eine Bananenschale.
Schritt 2: Brainstorming: Von wem könnte die Nachricht stammen? Welchen Inhalt hat die Nachricht? Hat die Bananenschale irgendwelche Folgen für Luke (z. B. Sturz)?
Schritt 3: Verfassen des Textes: Bringe deine Ideen als zusammenhängende Geschichte zu Papier. Schreibe im „Simple past" (z. B. receiv<u>ed</u>). Verwende auch die wörtliche Rede, um deine Geschichte lebendiger zu machen.

Beispiellösung:

A banana in the way

Luke was taking a walk in the park when he received a message from his brother Dave: "Sarah and I are getting married!" Luke smiled and wrote back: "Wow, that's great! When is the wedding?"
While he was looking at his mobile, Luke stepped on a banana peel on the path, slipped, almost fell to the ground and dropped his mobile. He heard the display crash and the mobile went out.
"That phone was new!" Luke moaned.
"Looks like this is not your lucky day," a young woman said smiling as she came towards him from the opposite direction.
"No, it's not." Luke replied. "My brother wanted to tell me about his wedding, but now my mobile is broken."
"I could lend you mine if you want to call him back." the woman said and handed him her phone. Luke was surprised but took it and smiled at her. He then noticed that the woman looked quite nice.
After Luke had made his call, he asked the woman if he could invite her for a coffee – and she said yes! In the end, the day turned into a lucky one for Luke!

(177 words)

Aufgabe 6

Hinweis: *Eine Bildergeschichte wie diese findest du häufig in der Abschlussprüfung. Betrachte in einem ersten Schritt die Bilder: die Keksdose ist leer, der Mann ist wütend, er schimpft die Katze, die Frau serviert die Kekse auf einem Tablett, der Mann bringt der Katze einen Kuchen. Verfasse nun deinen Text. Der Hauptteil, in dem der Mann zunächst die Katze verdächtigt und beschimpft, bis er herausfindet, dass er seinem Haustier Unrecht getan hat, sollte besonders ausgestaltet werden. Verwende dabei auch die wörtliche Rede sowie passende Adjektive und Adverbien.*

The suspect

Mr Smith wanted to have some biscuits at teatime. He looked into the biscuit box – but it was empty! Mr Smith grabbed his cat Kitty by the neck and showed her the empty box. He shouted: "You've eaten my biscuits!" Angrily, Mr Smith went to the kitchen to tell his wife that the biscuits were gone. Mrs Smith was preparing some tea and biscuits. Now he realised that his wife had emptied the biscuit box and not their cat! This made Mr Smith feel guilty, so he apologised to the cat for his bad behaviour by giving her a very yummy cake. *(102 words)*

Aufgabe 7

Hinweis: *Betrachte auch bei dieser Bildergeschichte zuerst die einzelnen Bilder und versuche, zu verstehen, was passiert: Junge Frau (Jenny) steigt in Zug, erhält während der Fahrt Textnachricht auf dem Smartphone, Freunde machen am Bahnsteig auf sich aufmerksam, Jenny verpasst die Haltestelle, sie sitzt an der nächsten Haltestelle und denkt daran, was die Freunde jetzt wohl machen. In deinem Text solltest du besonders auf Bild 4 eingehen, da es entscheidend für das Verständnis der Geschichte ist und den Höhepunkt ausmacht. Verwende in deiner Geschichte auch die wörtliche Rede. Der folgende Text ist eine Beispiellösung.*

One stop too far

On Saturday evening, Jenny got on the train to meet her friends at a party. She found a nice window seat, and started to use her smartphone. She wrote to her friends: "Meet you at 6 pm at Oldham Station. Looking forward to the party :-)" Then she switched to a game app. Jenny was so busy playing her game that she didn't notice the train arriving at Oldham Station. She also didn't see her friends, who came to meet her at the station and who were waving and shouting to catch her attention: "Jenny, get off the train!"; but Jenny was so concentrated on her game that she didn't see them.

It was 8 pm when Jenny sat on a bench at Weston Station. She was very unhappy that she had missed Oldham Station and now had to wait for the next train to take her back to Oldham. She thought of her friends, having a lot of fun at the party now, and she didn't look at her smartphone again that evening.

(174 words)

Aufgabe 8

Hinweis: *Diese Vorübung im Stil eines Austausches von Textnachrichten verlangt, dass du dich sowohl mit den Aussagen deiner englischsprachigen Chatpartnerin Jessy befasst, als auch auf die deutschen Vorgaben eingehst. Der Stil ist umgangssprachlich, d.h., Abkürzungen, die im Chat üblich sind, dürfen verwendet werden, z. B. TGIF (Thank God it's Friday).*

Jessy: Hi! I'm sorry for writing late. I'm just on my way to school. TGIF! How was your day?

Du: **My school day was OK. In the morning I had a test in English, which went well. I'm having a late lunch now and I'm going to meet my friends at the shopping mall later.**

Jessy: You're sooo lucky that you're already done with school for this week! My friend's having a sleepover party at her house tonight. Not sure if I'll go though. I don't feel well. What are your plans for the weekend?

Du: **My family is invited to my aunt's wedding on Sunday. I need a new dress for it, so that's why I'm going to the mall later.**

Jessy: Sounds great! You know, it's going to be so much fun once you come over to stay with us! By the way, my mom wants to know if there is any food that you don't like???

Du: **Thank your mom for asking! Honestly, I don't really like meat. I prefer vegetables and milk products. My mom showed me how to make a really great dish with potatoes, vegetables and cheese in the oven. If you like, I could show you how to make this when I am in Canada.**

Jessy: Sounds yummy! Anything else you'd like to know?

Du: **When I stay with your family, am I going to have my own room or am I going to share it with you? Do you think I could also go to a language course? I really want to improve my English.**
Is there a pool close to your house? I love swimming!
As a present for your parents I could bring some of my aunt's homemade honey. Do you think they would like that?

Jessy: Sorry! Have to get back to you later on all of that. We just arrived at school. Bye!

Aufgabe 9

Hinweis: *Bei dieser Vorübung zur Aufgabenvariante „Correspondence" ist die Struktur der Postkarte bereits durch Satzanfänge vorgegeben. Dies erleichtert dir das Schreiben. Beim Vervollständigen der Postkarte solltest du darauf achten, auf die deutschen Vorgaben einzugehen.*

3 January 20xx

Dear (aunt) Emily,

Best **wishes** from Johannesburg! I'm here with **mum and dad**. This place is **fantastic/great**! The weather is **hot and sunny** and I'm feeling **good/fantastic/great/wonderful/a bit tired because of the heat/ ...**
This is what we've already done in our holidays:
After arriving in Cape Town we spent a couple of days at a hotel at the beach. We also went sightseeing and shopping in the city, but the best part was the hike up to Lion's Head. We had a great view of the city and the ocean from there. On our last day in Cape Town Dad and I also did a surf course at False Bay and I was much better than him!
And we have further plans:
Tomorrow, we're going on a trip to Kruger National Park where we'll stay at a lodge. The day after we're going on a safari in the park. I really hope we'll see some big animals before we fly back home!

Love,
(your name)

Aufgabe 10

Hinweis: *Diese Aufgabe ist einer Aufgabe in der Prüfung schon recht ähnlich. Du bekommst eine E-Mail auf Englisch vorgelegt sowie zusätzliche Vorgaben auf Deutsch, die in deiner Antwort-Mail zu berücksichtigen sind. Lies zuerst, was Sean geschrieben hat, und kläre ggf. unbekannten Wortschatz, z. B. „to look for" = „suchen nach", „to wonder" = „sich fragen", „application" = „Bewerbung". Befasse dich dann mit den Vorgaben, die beim Erstellen der E-Mail aufzugreifen sind. Gehe sie der Reihe nach durch und schreibe zu jeder Vorgabe einen oder mehrere passende englische Sätze. Falls deine E-Mail dann noch nicht den nötigen Umfang hat, solltest du deinen Text entsprechend den Vorgaben weiter ausarbeiten oder eigene, passende Ideen einbringen (z. B. einen weiteren Vorschlag für eine gemeinsame Unternehmung). Die folgende E-Mail ist eine Beispiellösung.*

Hi Sean,

How are you? Thank you for your e-mail. I'm happy because I got a job at a hotel in Cambridge for the holidays. That's great, isn't it? I'll have to clean the rooms or support the staff at the reception, or help out in the kitchen. I'm glad that I'll earn some money. Afterwards I'll still have one week of my holidays left and I would love to spend it in Dublin with you. It would be a pity if I only worked during my holidays! I'd really like to come in the last week of August and I'm looking forward to the festival you told me about.

Take care,

(your name) *(113 words)*

Aufgabe 11

Hinweis: *Bei dieser „Correspondence"-Aufgabe bekommst du abgesehen von der englischen E-Mail keine weiteren inhaltlichen Vorgaben. Lies die Aufgabenstellung sowie die vorgegebene E-Mail zuerst sorgfältig durch. In der Prüfung kannst du unbekannte Wörter ggf. im Wörterbuch nachschlagen, z. B. „to guess" = „raten", „wildlife rescue station" = „Auffangstation für Wildtiere", „to drop somebody off" = „jemanden absetzen", „possum" = kleines australisches Beuteltier, „something matters" = „etwas ist wichtig/macht einen Unterschied".*
Beim Schreiben hast du relativ große Freiheit. Stelle jedoch stets einen Bezug zu Vanessas E-Mail her. Gehe z. B. auf ihren Wunsch ein, dir einmal alle Tiere zeigen zu können, und antworte auf ihre Fragen. Die folgende E-Mail ist eine Beispiellösung.

Dear Vanessa,

Thanks for your e-mail! You're so lucky that it's hot in Australia. It's freezing here in Germany and it has already snowed a little bit! My holidays are fine, but I have a cold ...
It sounds like you're having a wonderful internship at the wildlife rescue station. I would also like to do that. I think it's great that you help injured animals. Do they bite you sometimes? I hope not. Where did you find the baby camel? And how big is a baby camel?
I would also be happy if you could show the station and the animals to me someday. I've already asked my mom if I could get a trip to Australia for Christmas. She said it's too expensive, but I'm saving some money and maybe I'll be able to visit you in a year!

Take care,
(your name) *(143 words)*

Aufgabe 12 a

Hinweis: *Die Aufgaben 12 a und 12 b sind gelenkte Vorübungen zu Aufgabe 13. Die Angaben aus der Stellenanzeige sowie aus dem Bewerbungsformular (12 a) helfen dir, die Sätze im Bewerbungsschreiben (12 b) sinnvoll zu ergänzen. In der Prüfung musst du dann in der Lage sein, ein Bewerbungsschreiben auch ohne die oben genannten Hilfen zu verfassen. Lerne dazu den Aufbau eines Bewerbungsschreibens sowie typische Redewendungen (siehe 12 b) auswendig.*

Beispiellösung:

Name: Thomas (first) Bauer (last)

Gender: ☐ female ☒ male ☐ other

Date of birth: 7/8/20xx

Nationality: German

E-Mail: th.bauer@online.de

Position you want to apply for:
☒ receptionist ☐ room service ☐ kitchen help

Availability:
From: 1st (day) July (month) 20xx (year)
To: 31st (day) August (month) 20xx (year)

How many hours do you want to work per week?
☐ under 10 ☐ 10 – 20 ☒ 20 – 30 ☐ over 30

Preferred working period: ☒ mornings ☐ afternoons ☐ evenings

Do you have a valid driver's licence? ☐ yes ☒ no

Languages spoken: ☒ English ☐ French ☐ Spanish
☒ Others: German

Current occupation: ☒ student ☐ apprentice ☐ employed ☐ unemployed

Work experience:
internship in a small hotel

What makes you a true Oceanview Hotel staff member? I am …

☒ hard-working ☐ open-minded ☒ friendly ☐ helpful
☐ independent ☐ flexible ☒ ready to learn ☐ reliable
☐ skilful ☐ clever ☒ communicative ☐ sociable

Aufgabe 12 b

Hinweis: *Lies dir den Einleitungstext und die Anzeige genau durch. Die Angaben in der Anzeige helfen dir, die Sätze sinnvoll zu ergänzen. Du kannst dir als Hilfe für deine Ergänzungen auch noch einmal das Bewerbungsformular ansehen.*

Dear Mr Leary,

I saw your job advert **on the internet** and I am interested in working at **Ocean-view Hotel as a receptionist**. My name is ..., I am ... years old and I live in ..., Germany.
I am graduating from school in **June**. I have been learning English for **five** years and can speak it **well**. During my last summer holidays I **did an internship at a small hotel in my hometown**.
I am the right person for the job because **I am friendly and communicative**.
Working at your hotel would be a great opportunity for me to **gain some more experience**.
Could you please give me some more information about the job?
How long **would I have to work every day**? How much **do you pay**?

I look forward **to hearing from you**.

Yours sincerely,
(your name)

Aufgabe 13 a

Hinweis: *Die Aufgaben 13 a und 13 b erfordern ein Bewerbungsschreiben bzw. einen Lebenslauf (CV) in Tabellenform. Wenn dir das Verfassen eines Bewerbungsschreibens noch schwerfällt, bearbeite zunächst die Aufgaben 12 a und 12 b. Die folgende Lösung ist eine Beispiellösung.*

Dear Mrs Jackson,

I would like to apply for a job as a waiter/waitress at the River Café. My agency "Trips Down Under" suggested that I contact you.
I am 18 years old and I am soon going to finish my apprenticeship as a retail salesman/saleswoman at a department store. Before I start my first job I would like to gain some experience abroad and improve my English.
I am interested in the position of waiter/waitress because I enjoy working in service with customers and I also like working in a team.
I could start in November and stay for three months.

Finally, I would like to ask you how long I would have to work each day and how much I would earn.
I look forward to your reply.

Yours sincerely,

(your name)

Aufgabe 13 b

Hinweis: *Der folgende Lebenslauf ist ein Beispiel, an dem du dich orientieren kannst. Hier findest du auch typische Begriffe, die in einem Lebenslauf verwendet werden.*

CV

Personal information	Surname/Family name: Huber First name: Alexander Date of birth: 10 January 20xx Place of birth: Fürth/Germany
Education	• Middle school certificate • Apprentice as a retail salesman at Quick-Kauf department store in Erlangen
Practical experience	summer job as a waiter at Schlossgarten Café, Erlangen (3 weeks)
Skills	casual conversation with customers in English
Personal interests	sports (basketball, volleyball, running) dogs

Übungsaufgaben
Lösungen zum „Sprechen"

Allgemeiner Hinweis: *Du findest hier Aufgaben zu allen Bereichen der mündlichen Prüfung. Lies die Aufgabenstellungen genau durch, aber beachte, dass du sie in der Prüfung nicht vorgelegt bekommst, und die Aufgaben und Fragen ausschließlich mündlich an dich gerichtet werden. Beantworte alle Punkte möglichst ausführlich und begründe deine Antworten.*

Aufgabe 1

Hinweis: *Du hast hier 30 Sekunden Zeit, um das Foto zu betrachten und dir einen Überblick zu verschaffen, was auf dem Bild zu sehen ist. Achte auch schon auf Details (Wie viele Personen? Was ist zu sehen? Welche Situation? Etc.). Zunächst werden dir konkrete Fragen zum Bild gestellt, danach weiterführende Fragen. Versuche umfassend und logisch zu antworten. Du kannst natürlich jederzeit einen Blick auf das Bild werfen, um die gewünschten Informationen abzurufen.*

Beispiellösung:

a) I see a room. It is probably a music studio because a band is performing there, and it doesn't look like they're on a stage. The wall is white and has little holes in it. There is a window that looks out onto another room. I also see a long dark curtain. On the floor there might be a carpet.

b) There are four people – two young men and two young women – making music. The young man on the left is playing the keyboard. He is looking directly at the camera. The woman in the centre has her eyes closed while she is singing into the microphone. The guy on the right is playing an electric guitar. The girl at the back of the photo has raised her arms. She looks like she is about to strike the percussion instrument she is playing. Each of the musicians is smiling as they play their instruments.

c) All the musicians are wearing casual clothes. The two men are dressed in a similar way, and so are the two women. The guy with the guitar is wearing jeans and an undershirt, the other boy a T-shirt. The woman in the front is wearing torn dark trousers, a white T-shirt and a checked shirt. The drummer's shirt is the same style as the singer's.

d) I think it's more fun to make music when you're in a group. Doing something in a team is generally more fun than doing something on your own. As there are several instruments, the music becomes more interesting, too. Playing in a group is also a way to improve by learning from each other.

e) I like listening to pop music on the radio. My favourite station has a great mix of the latest hits in the morning. Listening to it helps start the day with energy.

Aufgabe 2

Hinweis: *Betrachte das Foto. Wie alt sind die dargestellten Personen ungefähr und welche Beziehung könnten sie zueinander haben? An welchem Ort könnte das Bild aufgenommen worden sein? Womit befassen die Jugendlichen sich gerade?*

Beispiellösung:

a) The four teenagers are outdoors. They're sitting on the ground and leaning against a low wall. In the background, there are the chairs of a café or restaurant. I think the young people are in a public place like a pedestrian zone.

b) Each of the teenagers has a smartphone in their hands. There's also a skateboard, which probably belongs to one of the boys. Next to each girl there is a bag.

c) It doesn't look like they are communicating with each other. Instead they are busy with their smartphones all by themselves. Maybe they are communicating with other people, writing messages to them, or they are using apps or playing games.

d) Yes, it looks like the four young people are good friends. They are sitting close to each other on the pavement. The arms of the boy and girl in the middle are touching, and the boy in the middle has also put his arm behind the boy on the right. They also have a similar style of clothing (leather jackets and denim jeans, for example), which is often typical of good friends.

e) Both things are important: Meeting friends personally and staying in contact with them via messages or social networks. When I meet my friends, we can talk face to face, make jokes, laugh and have a lot of fun together. I can look at my friends' faces and see how they are feeling, or give them a hug when they are sad or worried. It is not possible to have the same kind of experience when your friends are not around in person. But I also don't want to do without staying in touch with my friends online. The advantage is that we can communicate even if we are far apart from each other or if we're busy with other things. It can also be fun to text each other and make jokes that way, or to send each other selfies of where we are at the moment.

Aufgabe 3

Hinweis: *Sieh dir den Werbespot an. Welche Personen kommen vor? Mit welchem Problem wird der Mann konfrontiert? Wie löst er das Problem? Ist der Spot ernst oder humorvoll? An welche Zielgruppe könnte er sich richten? Wozu wird der Zuschauer (indirekt) aufgefordert?*

Beispiellösung:

Scene description: In the video you see a father carrying his little daughter to the car. When they have almost reached the car, the girl shows her father that her doll has lost a shoe. This makes the father go back over the hot sand to pick it up.

a) He desperately wants to reach his car because he is walking barefoot on hot sand and carrying his daughter as well as lots of beach equipment. He is suffering because of his heavy load, and because the hot sand and the pebbles on the car park make his feet hurt.

b) The doll has lost its shoe on the way from the beach to the car. It is now lying somewhere in the hot sand.

c) The father is unhappy because he realizes that he will have to go back to fetch the shoe, but when his daughter looks at him hopefully, he knows he has got to go back.

d) Yes, the father behaves like a superhero because first he has to walk on the hot sand to take his daughter and the beach equipment to the parking lot, and then he turns around again to go back to fetch the doll's shoe. He also doesn't leave his daughter by the car but takes her with him to get the shoe. When he turns around to go down the beach again, the wind blows up the beach towel that is wrapped around his neck, making it look like the cape of a superhero.

e) The message behind the car being "for real superheros" probably refers to parents who would do anything for their family and children. These parents are the ones who deserve this car, which is only for special people. While a superhero from a comic is a fictional character with supernatural powers (e. g. Batman, Spiderman, etc.) a "real" superhero according to this video clip is the ordinary, loving father, who does everything for his child.

Aufgabe 4

Hinweis: *Hier findest du eine Beispiellösung zu jedem Stichwort in der Mindmap. In der Prüfung musst du jedoch nur drei Stichpunkte wählen und dazu deinen Vortrag halten. Vergiss nicht, deinem Vortrag eine Struktur zu geben, z. B. folgendermaßen: "My topic is …", "The keywords I've chosen are …", "I'll start with …"*

Beispiellösung:

Good morning! I'm giving a talk about New Zealand today. I'll start with the country's **geography**: New Zealand is situated in the South Pacific. It mainly consists of two islands, the North Island and the South Island. New Zealand is far away from other countries: its closest neighbour, Australia, is about 2 000 km away. The capital of New Zealand is Wellington with about 200 000 inhabitants. The largest city is Auckland in the very north with a population of about 1.5 million people.

Next, I'm going to tell you something about New Zealand's **climate and landscape**. The country lies in different climatic zones, ranging from wet to dry climates. There are rainforests, for example, and mountain areas. On the South Island you can spend a sunny day at the beach in the morning and go skiing in the afternoon. In the south, there are also spectacular fjords and high mountains, which are called the "Southern Alps". New Zealand is also known for its many volcanoes and earthquakes because it lies at the boundary of two tectonic plates.

Now to the country's **native population**, the Māori. They arrived from the Polynesian islands in the South Pacific in the 14th century. About 300 years later the first Europeans came to New Zealand, and from the 19th century mainly people from Britain settled there. Today most New Zealanders are of European origin, while the Māori are the country's largest minority with 16.5 % of the population. Māori culture has now become an important part of New Zealand's identity. A lot of places in New Zealand have Māori names. The Māori word for New Zealand is "Aotearoa", which means "land of the long white cloud".

The Māori **language** is one of New Zealand's official languages and it is spoken by about 4 % of the population. The other official languages are English and New Zealand Sign Language. New Zealand has its own accent of English, which is similar to Australian English. Other examples of languages spoken in New Zealand are Mandarin Chinese and Hindi.

Tourism is very important for New Zealand. The country's various landscapes offer the opportunity for lots of different types of sports and leisure activities. You can go hiking, skiing and rock climbing in the mountains, for example, or you can relax at the beach. The country is also perfect for water sports like sailing, kayaking or rafting. Of course, the most famous attraction is bungy jumping, which was invented in New Zealand. There are also many caves to explore. For "Lord of the Rings" and "The Hobbit" fans it is a must to visit the places where the movies were filmed, for example the Hobbiton™ movie set.

Finally, I'd like to share some facts about **animals** in New Zealand. As New Zealand was isolated from the rest of the world for millions of years, there are animals that can be found only there. The country's most famous animal is the kiwi, a flightless bird. By the way, New Zealanders also call themselves "kiwis" and the kiwi fruit also gets its name from this bird because it is so fuzzy. New Zealand also has a lot of sheep – there are about six sheep for every person in the country!

Aufgabe 5

Hinweis: *Du findest hier eine Beispiellösung zu allen sechs Aspekten. In der Prüfung sprichst du nur zu drei Stichwörtern.*

Beispiellösung „Topic-based talk":

I'd like to give a talk about the topic "holidays". My first keyword is holiday **destinations**. In summertime, many people want to travel. Typical destinations are the sea, the mountains or interesting cities. Most people like to travel with their families or in groups to have a better experience. Those who go to the sea often lie on the beach, spending long hours in the sun. Beach holidays are the most popular holiday with children. Others prefer the mountains and the many possibilities of exercise they offer, such as hiking, mountain biking, rock climbing or skiing in the winter. I'm dreaming of spending a holiday with my best friends at a resort in Florida.

My second point is **transport**, so it's about how you can reach your holiday destination. The classic way of travelling is by car. This is the easiest way to transport one's belongings to the holiday location, but in order to reach distant places, most travellers also take a plane. While travelling by train is a popular option for city tours, other tourists like to go on holiday on ship cruises.

Now I'd like to give some information about holiday **seasons**. You can go on a holiday all year round, but the season you want to go on holiday depends on what you want to do. A lot of people like to go on holiday in summer, but it is not the only time of the year that's great for vacations. Lovers of winter sports wait all year until it finally gets cold. The Alps, for example are great for skiing, snowboarding and sledding. City tours, for example to Paris and Rome, are usually best in spring and autumn when it's neither too hot nor too cold.

What do **languages** have to do with holidays? Well, if you don't stay in your home country, you have to be prepared to communicate with people who speak another language. Tourists usually get along with English all over the world. In most western countries, English is spoken by many people, especially by service personnel in hotels or holiday resorts. The adventurous travel to exotic places where communication can be a challenge. Still the experience can be great.

Finally, I want to talk about **problems** while you are on holiday. Many things can go wrong during a holiday trip. Getting ill is the most frequent and annoying

thing. Sometimes the problems start before you have reached your destination – you can miss a plane, your car can break down or you realise that your passport isn't valid any more. Depending on where you're heading, local crime can also be an issue.
An important aspect is **cultural differences**, which sometimes need getting used to, like dress codes for women in Arabic countries. Therefore it is good to be well-informed about local customs before going on holiday.

Aufgabe 6

Hinweis: *In der Prüfung wird der Dialog üblicherweise Satz für Satz von den beiden Prüfenden vorgelesen, du selbst erhältst keine Textvorlage. Die Verwendung der indirekten Rede („Er/Sie sagt …") ist nicht nötig. Übertrage sinngemäß vom Englischen ins Deutsche und umgekehrt. Du musst also nicht wortwörtlich übersetzen. Manchmal bietet es sich an, Wörter oder Ausdrücke zu umschreiben. Versuche zügig zu übersetzen und die Zeitvorgabe von fünf Minuten pro Dialog einzuhalten. Die folgenden Lösungen sind Beispiele.*

Good morning. What can I do for you?

Guten Morgen. Was kann ich für Sie tun?

Also ich habe ein Problem mit meinem Fuß. Er tut so weh.

I have a problem with my foot. It really hurts.

Where does it hurt exactly? Could you show me, please?

Wo tut es genau weh? Könnten Sie es mir zeigen?

Hier unten. Die Haut ist auch schon rot.

Down here. The skin is also red. / The skin has also turned red.

Have you had this problem before?

Hatten Sie dieses Problem schon einmal?

Ich glaube nicht. Es ist neu.

I don't think so. It's new.

What about your shoes? Is your shoe scratching or rubbing against your skin?

Was ist mit Ihren Schuhen? Kratzt oder reibt der Schuh auf der Haut?

Nein. Meine Schuhe sind wirklich bequem.

No, they aren't. My shoes are really comfortable.

Well, I think you should see a doctor. There is a very good one next door. Why don't you go there?

Also ich denke, Sie sollten zum Arzt gehen. Nebenan gibt es einen sehr guten. Warum gehen Sie nicht dahin?/Gehen Sie doch dorthin.

Das ist eine gute Idee. Das mache ich. Vielen Dank.

That's a good idea. I'll do that. Thank you very much./Thanks a lot.

Get well soon and goodbye!

Gute Besserung und auf Wiedersehen.

Aufgabe 7

Hinweis: *Übertrage wieder vom Englischen ins Deutsche und umgekehrt. Auch hier musst du, wie auch in den folgenden Aufgaben, die Perspektive nicht wechseln.*

Good afternoon. What can I do for you?

Guten Tag. Was kann ich für Sie tun? / Wie kann ich Ihnen helfen? /
Schmidt, guten Tag. Ich habe eine Reservierung.

Good afternoon/Hello. My name is Schmidt/I'm Mr. Schmidt. I've made a reservation.

Mr. Schmidt. Your reservation is from 15th to 18th August. Could I have your passport and your credit card, please?

Herr Schmidt, Ihre Reservierung ist vom 15. bis zum 18. August. Könnte ich bitte Ihren Pass/Ausweis und Ihre Kreditkarte haben?

Hier, bitte. Können Sie mich morgen um 6 Uhr wecken?

Here you are. Could you please wake me up tomorrow at 6 a.m./6 o'clock in the morning?

Sure! Here's your key. Your room is number 223. Breakfast is served from 6 to 10 a.m. The breakfast room is on the first floor.

Natürlich/Gerne. Hier ist Ihr Schlüssel. Ihr Zimmer hat die Nummer 223. Von 6 Uhr bis 10 Uhr gibt es Frühstück. Der Frühstücksraum befindet sich im Erdgeschoss.

Habe ich von meinem Zimmer aus einen schönen Ausblick über die Stadt oder kann ich die Freiheitsstatue sehen?

Do I have a nice view of the city from my room, or can I see the Statue of Liberty?

Sorry, your room is on the second floor. So there really isn't much of a view, but I think you'll still like your room because it is pretty quiet. You know, quiet rooms are not so typical for New York.

Es tut mir leid, aber Ihr Zimmer ist im zweiten Stock. Deshalb haben Sie dort nicht wirklich viel Aussicht. Aber ich denke, dass Sie das Zimmer trotzdem mögen werden, weil es ziemlich ruhig (gelegen) ist. Wissen Sie, ruhige Zimmer sind für New York nicht typisch.

Kein Problem. Kann ich im Hotel Tickets für das Musical „Lion King“ kaufen?

No problem. Can I buy tickets for the musical "Lion King" at the hotel?

I'm sorry we don't sell theatre tickets. You can buy them at the theatres on Broadway or at the ticket office on Times Square.

Es tut mir leid. / Leider nein. Wir verkaufen keine Theaterkarten. Sie können diese in den Theatern am Broadway oder am Ticketstand am Times Square kaufen.

Danke! Auf Wiedersehen.

Thank you! Goodbye.

Aufgabe 8

Hinweis: *Dolmetsche zwischen der deutschen Touristin und der Verkäuferin.*

Hello, can I help you?

Hallo, (wie) kann ich Ihnen helfen?

Ja, bitte. Ich hätte gerne dieses blaue T-Shirt in L.

Yes, I'd like to have the blue T-shirt in size L / Large, please. /
Could you give me this blue T-shirt in large, please?

Here you are.

Hier, bitte schön.

Wo kann ich es anprobieren?

Where can I try it on?

The changing rooms are over there.

Die Umkleidekabinen sind dort drüben.

(Nach dem Anprobieren). Dieses T-Shirt ist zu groß. Kann ich ein kleineres haben?

This T-shirt is too large (for me). Could I have a smaller one, please?

Of course. Here it is.

Ja, natürlich. Hier bitte.

(Nach dem Anprobieren). Jetzt passt es. Wie viel kostet es?

This one fits. How much is it?

It's £ 20. Would you like anything else?

(Es kostet) 20 Pfund. Brauchen Sie sonst noch etwas?/Kann ich sonst noch etwas für Sie tun?

Ich nehme noch diese beiden Postkarten. Verkaufen Sie auch Briefmarken?

I'd like these postcards, please. Do you also sell stamps?

No, I'm sorry. You have to buy them at the post office.

Leider nein./Es tut mir leid. Die müssen Sie im Postamt kaufen.

Schade. Trotzdem danke und auf Wiedersehen.

What a pity. Anyway, thank you. Goodbye.

Aufgabe 9

Hinweis: *Da dein englischer Freund mit deiner Oma vermutlich nicht bekannt ist, solltest du die höfliche „Sie"-Form verwenden.*

Hi, would you like me to give you my opinion on a computer game?

Hallo, möchten Sie, dass ich Ihnen meine Meinung zu einem Computerspiel sage/Sie zu einem Computerspiel berate?

Ja, das wäre toll!

That would be great.

What questions do you have?

Welche Fragen haben Sie?

Mitschüler haben meinem Enkel dieses Spiel hier empfohlen, aber ich weiß nicht viel darüber. Kannst du mir etwas dazu sagen?

Classmates recommended this game to my grandson, but I don't know much about it. Can/Could you tell me more about, please?

Of course. It's new on the market and a very good game. You can also play it online.

Natürlich. Es ist neu auf dem Markt und ein sehr gutes Spiel. Man kann es auch online spielen.

Das klingt gut. Ich bin mir sicher, dass es ihm gefallen wird. Aber was bedeutet „online"?

That sounds good. I'm sure he'll like it, but what does "online" mean?

It means that you can play it together with your friends on the computer without meeting them in person.

Das bedeutet, dass man es zusammen mit Freunden auf dem Computer spielen kann, ohne dass man sich persönlich trifft.

Aha. Er hat mir auch erzählt, dass es in dem Spiel viele Funktionen gibt. Man kann z. B. kochen und die Kleidung seines Charakters ändern.

I see. He also told me that there are a lot of functions/features in the game. You can cook or change the clothes of the characters, for example.

That's right. You can also own a pet and fight with a sword.

Das ist richtig. Man kann auch ein Haustier besitzen und mit einem Schwert kämpfen.

Das klingt aufregend. Du hast mir sehr geholfen. Ich kaufe es ihm bestimmt und ich hoffe, dass er viel Spaß damit haben wird.

That sounds exciting. You helped me a lot. I'm definitely going to buy it for him. I hope he'll have lots of fun with it.

Aufgabe 10

Hinweis: *Dolmetsche zwischen der australischen Austauschschülerin und deiner kleinen Schwester.*

Hi Emma! My name is Jasmin. I go to school here in Australia. Do you go to school yet?

Hi Emma! Ich heiße Jasmin. Ich gehe hier in Australien zur Schule. Gehst du schon in die Schule?

Ich gehe in die 2. Klasse, aber ich habe noch kein Englisch in der Schule. Lernst du auch Deutsch?

I'm in 2nd grade/class 2, but I haven't had English in school, yet. Do you also learn German?/Are you also learning German?

I only had one year of German, but I really didn't learn much. I hope my German will improve when I stay with you.

Ich hatte nur ein Jahr Deutsch, aber ich habe nicht wirklich viel gelernt. Ich hoffe, dass mein Deutsch besser wird, wenn ich bei euch wohne.

Super, dann kannst du mit mir deutsch sprechen und ich kann dir alle Wörter erklären.

Great, then you can speak German with me and I can explain all the words to you.

That's a very nice offer! And of course I can help you learn English too.

Das ist ein sehr nettes Angebot. Und ich kann dir natürlich auch helfen, Englisch zu lernen.

Das wäre toll! Hast du daheim eigentlich auch ein Känguru?

That would be great! By the way, do you also have a kangaroo at home?

We don't keep kangaroos as pets, but the house is surrounded by bushland and sometimes kangaroos come to our place.

Wir halten keine Kängurus als Haustiere, aber um unser Haus herum ist sehr viel Busch(land), und Kängurus kommen manchmal zu uns (aufs Grundstück).

Füttert ihr denn die Kängurus?

Do you also feed the kangaroos?

No way! It's bad for wild animals if they're fed and they should not get used to coming to our place.

Auf keinen Fall! Es ist schlecht für Wildtiere, wenn man sie füttert und sie sollten sich auch nicht daran gewöhnen, zu uns (nach Hause) zu kommen.

Das ist schade. Ich würde mich freuen, wenn ich ein Känguru im Garten hätte!

What a pity. I'd be happy to have a kangaroo in my garden.

Aufgabe 11

Hinweis: *Da Influencer*innen sich meist locker und umgangssprachlich ausdrücken, ist es natürlich, die „Du-Form" zu benutzen.*

Hi, I heard you wanted my advice?

Hallo, ich habe gehört, dass du gerne meinen Rat hättest.

Ja, denn ich verbringe viel Zeit zu Hause vor dem Computer, weshalb ich gerne mehr Sport machen möchte. Kannst du mir Tipps geben?

Yes, I spend too much time on my computer, which is why I'd like to do more sport(s). Can you give me some tips, please?

Yes, of course. There's a lot you can do.

Ja natürlich. Es gibt vieles, was du tun kannst.

Ich bin ein großer Fan von dir und hätte auch gerne so einen perfekten Körper.

I'm a big fan of yours and I'd also like to have such a perfect body.

But it's your personality that really counts. Sports is a good way though to improve your health and wellbeing.

Aber es ist deine Persönlichkeit, die wirklich zählt. Sport ist allerdings eine gute Möglichkeit, deine Gesundheit und dein Wohlbefinden zu verbessern.

Was könntest du mir vorschlagen? Meine Schwester, zum Beispiel, spielt Basketball in einem Verein.

What could you suggest? My sister, for example, plays basketball in a club.

Joining a club is a great way to get out of the house and make new friends!

Ein Sportverein ist eine tolle Möglichkeit, aus dem Haus zu kommen und neue Freunde zu finden!

Das klingt gut, aber gibt es auch irgendwelche Übungen, die ich zu Hause machen kann?

That sounds good, but are there also some exercises that I could do at home?

Sure. Have a look at my channel – you'll find a lot of motivating exercises there.

Na klar. Schau mal in meinen Kanal rein, dort wirst du viele motivierende Übungen finden.

Danke, das werde ich tun! Jetzt fühle ich mich besser, weil ich ein paar Ideen habe.

Thanks, I'll do that. Now I feel much better because I have some ideas.

Aufgabe 12

Hinweis: *Übertrage das Gespräch zwischen deinen beiden Freunden/Freundinnen vom Englischen ins Deutsche und umgekehrt.*

Hi, nice to meet you!

Hallo, schön dich kennenzulernen!

Hallo! Ich bin froh, dass ich mit dir reden kann. Ich habe die Schule abgeschlossen und weiß nicht, welchen Beruf ich jetzt ausüben soll.

Hi! I'm happy that I can talk to you. I've finished school and I don't know what kind of job I should do now.

I feel the same. I want to start working and not go to school again.

Mir geht es auch so. Ich will anfangen zu arbeiten und nicht wieder in die Schule gehen.

Ich finde, dass man in der Schule viel lernen kann.

I think you can learn a lot at school.

I found school rather boring.

Ich finde, dass die Schule ziemlich langweilig war.

Das ist schade zu hören. Wieso?

That's a pity to hear. Why?

I always had bad grades, but I like sports, so maybe I could become a fitness trainer.

Ich hatte immer schlechte Noten, aber ich mag Sport. Deshalb könnte ich vielleicht Fitnesstrainer*in werden.

Das klingt gut, aber für mich wäre das nichts.

That sounds good, but I wouldn't do this personally.

Right. So, I guess you had really good grades at school?

OK, also nehme ich an, dass du wirklich gute Noten in der Schule hattest.

In der Schule war ich gut in Mathe und Biologie. Und ich helfe gerne anderen.

At school, I was good at maths and biology and I like helping others.

If I were you, I'd become a medical assistant or nurse.

An deiner Stelle würde ich Medizinische*r Fachangestellte*r oder Krankenpfleger*in werden.

Ja, das wäre interessant. Ich werde mal darüber nachdenken, bevor ich eine Entscheidung treffe.

Yes, that would be interesting. I'll think about it before making a decision.

Qualifizierender Abschluss der Mittelschule Bayern
Lösungen – Offizielle Musteraufgabe Englisch

A Hör- und Hörsehverstehen

Allgemeiner Hinweis: *In der Prüfung werden die Hörtexte jeweils zweimal vorgespielt. In den Pausen vor und nach den Texten hast du Zeit, um die Aufgaben durchzulesen bzw. die Lösungen einzutragen. Du darfst dabei ein gedrucktes Wörterbuch verwenden – denke aber an die knappe Arbeitszeit. Beachte, dass ab dem Quali 2022 auch im Hörverstehen bei Rechtschreibfehlern Punkte abgezogen werden.*

Aufgabe 1

Flight Captain: Good afternoon, ladies and gentlemen. This is captain Tom McBrain speaking.
I'd like to inform you that the arrival of our flight, BS389 in Gibraltar will be delayed by about 15 minutes because of the bad weather we had half an hour after our departure from London Heathrow. So, our time of arrival will be about four forty-five pm.
That was the bad news I had to tell you, and now the good news.
As you might already know, Gibraltar Airport is not the easiest airport at which to land. There are often strong cross-winds which the pilot has to deal with. In the past, some aircraft have had to travel on to Malaga, but today we're lucky. There's hardly any wind. The weather is calm and dry, so we expect a smooth landing.
At the moment, the temperature in Gibraltar is 21 degrees Celsius, which is 69.8 degrees Fahrenheit. We will start our descent soon and will be landing shortly. If you take a look outside on the right of our aircraft as we approach for landing, you might be able to see the famous Monkey Rock and another frequently visited sight in Gibraltar, the Europa Point Lighthouse, which is the southernmost lighthouse in Europe.
Ladies and gentlemen, please return to your seats now, fasten your seat belts and make sure that the tables in front of you are in an upright position …

Hinweis: *Für jede vollständig richtige Lösung bekommst du hier einen Punkt. Du musst nicht in ganzen Sätzen antworten.*

1. (at) 4:45 (pm) / four forty-five (pm / in the afternoon)
   Hinweis: *Z. 5 f.*

2. (strong) cross-winds
   Hinweis: *Z. 9*
3. (there's) hardly any wind / calm and dry weather
   Hinweis: *Z. 11 f.*
4. 21 degrees Celsius / 21 °C / 69.8 degrees Fahrenheit / 69.8 °F
   Hinweis: *Z. 13 f.*
5. (on the) right (side)
   Hinweis: *Z. 15 ff.*

Aufgabe 2

Taxi driver: Good afternoon, Madam, where can I take you to?

Mother: Hello, Europe Street, please. We've booked a room in the Monkey Rock Hotel.

Susan: Does it take a long time to get there?

Taxi driver: No, Miss, it's only about five kilometres. I guess fifteen minutes or so.

Mike: Fifty minutes? I didn't know traffic in Gibraltar was that slow.

Mother: Mike, take off those headphones, so that you can understand what people are saying.

Taxi driver: There are two routes. Would you prefer the eastern or the western one?

Mike & Susan: What's the difference?

Taxi driver: The western route is the more historical route, where you'll be able to see some historical buildings Gibraltar has to offer, whereas on the eastern route you can see more landscape, some of Gibraltar's best beaches and the best-known sight, the Rock of Gibraltar.

Mike & Susan: Ah, Mum, not history again. Let's take the eastern route.

Mother: Yes, that sounds interesting. Is this the rock where those famous Gibraltar monkeys live?

Taxi driver: That's right, madam, but the rock also offers a breathtaking view over the port and the sea. I'd recommend a guided tour to visit the rock. You'll learn something about the history of Gibraltar and, if the weather conditions are good, it will be possible to get a view across the Strait of Gibraltar to Africa.

Susan: Oh Mum, we must do that, please.

Mike: Yeah, cool, we'll be able to get close to Africa, wow.

Mother: Anything else you would say is a must on this route?

Taxi driver: Well, there are some popular beaches. Catalan Bay, for example, has a nice beach, small hotels and some restaurants and pubs. All in all, I would say a quieter place for a holiday. Sandy Bay has become a popular beach again since 2014.

Mike: Why do you say it has become a popular beach again?

Taxi driver: Some years ago, there was a strong Atlantic storm. The waves were high and powerful. And most of the sand of Sandy Beach was washed away. Then the authorities wanted to make the bay sandy again. More than 50,000 tons of sand were imported from the western Sahara and wave-breakers were built to prevent the sand from being washed away again.

Mother: Hmm … that's interesting.

Susan: Yeah, that's good to know, too. I like a place where I can relax on a nice beach and go swimming.

Taxi driver: Well, the best place in my opinion would be Sandy Bay. OK, we'll be soon arriving at your hotel. It's just around the next corner on the left hand side after the traffic lights …

Hinweis: *Für jede richtige Lösung erhältst du einen Punkt. Streichst du mehr Wörter bei einer Teilaufgabe durch, bekommst du keinen Punkt.*

1. It's only about ~~fifty~~ kilometres away.
   Hinweis: *Z. 5*
2. The western ~~road~~ is more historical.
   Hinweis: *Z. 11*
3. The ~~port~~ offers a breathtaking view.
   Hinweis: *Z. 18*
4. You'll learn something about the ~~environment~~ of Gibraltar.
   Hinweis: *Z. 19 f.*
5. Since 2014 Sandy Bay has become a ~~private~~ beach again.
   Hinweis: *Z. 27*
6. A strong storm washed away ~~some~~ of the sand of Sandy Bay.
   Hinweis: *Z. 31*

Aufgabe 3

Tour Guide: Welcome on board the "Queen of Gibraltar". I'm Rufo López, your guide on our three-hour whale-watching trip.
Whales are absolutely wonderful creatures, big and elegant. They're amongst the most interesting animals on our earth. If we're lucky we'll be able to see dolphins as well as killer whales, which you might know as orcas. So put on your life vests and let's get out to sea to meet the whales.
Ladies and gentlemen, our captain has switched off the engine and we're just drifting with the ocean current. If you look to the right you can see a group of dolphins accompanying our boat. Dolphins can be between 1.7 and 2.3 metres long, weigh up to 135 kilograms, swim very fast, about 65 km/h, and live 35 to 40 years.

Susan: Wow, look, Mike, it looks as if they're a whole family.

Tour Guide: Look to the left now. There is a whale, about a kilometre away. Through the binoculars it looks like a huge orca. Maybe we'll get the chance to see it at closer range.

Mother: Oh, I like orcas. They're so graceful and grand. They always look so peaceful …

Tour Guide: Orcas grow up to a length of 10 metres and can be really heavy, between 1.6 and 9 tons. They live longer than dolphins. Female orcas can even live to be 80 years old.

Mother: I remember a TV series when I was a little girl with a very intelligent dolphin named Flipper.

Tour Guide: Oh yes, dolphins are very intelligent and have very good hearing. They produce lots of different sounds like clicks and whistles to communicate. They even have names for each other; but orcas are clever as well.
The orcas, also called killer whales, here in the Strait of Gibraltar have developed a special hunting technique which really annoys fishermen around here. Orcas like tuna very much and if a fisherman has got one on the hook of his fishing line and is trying to pull it out of the water, the orca waits patiently until the tuna is only 20 metres below the surface and then bites off the body of the fish and eats it. What the poor fisherman finally reels onto his boat is only the head of the tuna with the hook in its mouth.

Mike: Ah, they really are clever creatures!

Tour Guide: Now we'll restart the engine and move on to another place where we usually have a good chance of meeting some pilot whales who are migrating through this area at this time of the year …

Hinweis: *Um die Tabelle richtig zu vervollständigen musst du genau darauf hören, ob gerade von den Orcas oder den Delfinen die Rede ist. Es gibt auf jede komplett richtige Antwort einen Punkt.*

1. 65
   Hinweis: *Z. 10*
2. 80
   Hinweis: *Z. 19 f.*
3. hear
   Hinweis: *Z. 23*
4. sounds
   Hinweis: *Z. 23 f.*
5. names
   Hinweis: *Z. 24 f.*
6. hunting
   Hinweis: *Z. 26 f.*
7. hook of a fisherman's fishing line / fishing lines / fishermen
   Hinweis: *Z. 28 ff.*

B Sprachgebrauch

Allgemeiner Hinweis: *In diesem Prüfungsteil liegt der Schwerpunkt auf Wortschatz und Grammatik. Bei Rechtschreibfehlern werden dir Punkte abgezogen (Ausnahmen gelten bei anerkannter Rechtschreibstörung). Ein zweisprachiges gedrucktes Wörterbuch ist erlaubt.*

Aufgabe 1

Hinweis: *Hier musst du ohne Vorgaben das jeweils passende Wort einsetzen. Lies dir den Text mit den Lücken erst einmal ganz durch, damit du verstehst, um was es inhaltlich geht. In den Lückensätzen kannst du durch den Textzusammenhang oder bestimmte Wörter erkennen, welches Wort du einsetzen musst.*

1. *Steht im* if*-Satz das Verb im Präsens, wird im Hauptsatz das „will-future" verwendet.*
2. *much/a lot/far more = „viel mehr"*
3. *Hier muss das „present perfect" verwendet werden, da es sich um einen Zeitraum von 1713 (Signalwort „since" = „seit") bis heute handelt.*

4. *„one of the UK's 14 overseas territories" = „eines von Großbritanniens 14 Überseeterritorien"*
5. *Steigerung: „not more than" = „nicht mehr als"*
6. *Possessivbegleiter: „the territory has its own flag" = „das Territorium hat seine eigene Flagge"*
7. *„public holiday" = „gesetzlicher Feiertag"*
8. *„dress in red and white" = „sich in Rot und Weiß kleiden"*
9. *„drive/travel on the right-hand side" = „auf der rechten Seite fahren"*

If you ask people (0) about Gibraltar, most of them (1) **will** tell you about the monkeys. But this bit of land near the southern tip of Spain offers (2) **much / a lot / far** more than a big rock with monkeys on it.
Gibraltar (3) **has been** part of the United Kingdom since 1713. It is (4) **one** of the UK's 14 overseas territories. Although the land itself is not more (5) **than** 6.7 square kilometres in area, it is strategically important and the British are determined not to give it back to Spain.
The territory has (6) **its** own flag and the National Day, September 10, is a public (7) **holiday** in Gibraltar. On this day the inhabitants all dress (8) **in** red and white, which are their national colours. English is the official language of this crown colony but Spanish and a local dialect are spoken as well.
In Gibraltar, unlike most other UK overseas territories, all the cars, buses and bikes (9) **drive/travel** on the right-hand side of the road. All in all, Gibraltar is a melting pot of many cultures.

Aufgabe 2

Hinweis: *Bei dieser Aufgabe sollst du das vorgegebene Wort so verändern, dass es in den Satz passt. Meist musst du die Wortart (Nomen, Verb, Adjektiv etc.) ändern bzw. ein anderes Wort aus der Wortfamilie nehmen. Dies kannst du durch den Satzzusammenhang herausfinden. Beachte dabei z. B. bei Verben auch die richtige Zeitform.*

1. *decided: Verb im „simple past"*
2. *flight (Nomen): „einen Flug buchen"*
3. *Im Zusammenhang mit „mass" passt hier nur „tourism" = „Massentourismus"*
4. *attraction (Nomen) = „Attraktion/Sehenswürdigkeit"*
5. *location (Nomen) = „Ort"*
6. *surprised (Adjektiv): „wir waren überrascht"*
7. *Hier geht es um die Personen, die die Musik machen = „musicians"*

8. *In diesem Fall gibt es zwei Möglichkeiten: die Musiker*innen sind Studierende (Nomen: „students") oder sie üben fleißig (Adverb: „studiously practising")*
9. *bored (Adjektiv): „wir waren nicht gelangweilt" / „uns war nicht langweilig"*

Last November my family and I wanted to escape the rainy (0) British winter. So we (1) **decided** to go on a short trip south and booked a (2) **flight** from Manchester to Gibraltar. As we don't like mass (3) **tourism** we did not visit the Monkey Rock, the most famous (4) **attraction**. Instead we went to the Botanic Gardens, a place I would recommend to everyone. The gardens and plant houses make it a wonderful (5) **location** which can be hired for special events like marriages and receptions. While walking around we were really (6) **surprised** to see (7) **musicians** playing in the middle of a beautiful arrangement of plants. They were (8) **students / studiously** practising for their next concert in the Botanic Gardens. All in all, Gibraltar is not really that different from Britain. In our opinion it is quite interesting. We were not (9) **bored** at all. Our break was short, but it was very enjoyable.

C Leseverstehen

Allgemeiner Hinweis: *In diesem Prüfungsteil wird dein Leseverständnis geprüft, indem du Aufgaben zum allgemeinen und detaillierten Verständnis bearbeitest. Es ist dabei sinnvoll, vorher bereits den Umgang mit dem Wörterbuch zu üben, sodass du nicht so viel Zeit zum Nachschlagen brauchst. Versuche auch, Wörter aus dem Textzusammenhang zu erschließen.*
Verschaffe dir beim ersten Lesen einen Überblick, worum es im Text geht. Beim zweiten Lesen solltest du den Inhalt möglichst genau verstehen. Markiere dabei diejenigen Stellen im Text, auf die sich die jeweilige Aufgabe bezieht.

Aufgabe 1

Hinweis: *Hier musst die vorgegebenen Überschriften (1–8) den einzelnen Textabschnitten (A–F) zuordnen. Zwei Überschriften passen dabei nicht.*

A	B	C	D	E	F
1	2	4	8	6	5

Aufgabe 2

Hinweis: *Für jede vollständig richtige Lösung bekommst du hier einen Punkt. Du musst nicht in ganzen Sätzen antworten.*

1. (the) (Moorish) Castle
   Hinweis: *Z. 12*
2. (by) cable car
   Hinweis: *Z. 18*
3. (migrating) birds
   Hinweis: *Z. 20 f.*
4. (too much) human interaction
   Hinweis: *Z. 30*
5. (the) Shard (in London)/London's tallest skyscraper
   Hinweis: *Z. 41 f.*
6. (the weight of) five (Asian) elephants/340 people
   Hinweis: *Z. 44*

Aufgabe 3

Hinweis: *Lies dir noch einmal die Abschnitte D und E durch und bringe die Ereignisse in die Reihenfolge, in der sie geschehen sind. Dass einige Affen nach Spanien gegeben wurden, kommt im Text nicht vor.*

The monkeys lived only in Africa.	**1**
Some monkeys were sent on to Spain.	–
Today's monkey population is doing fine.	6
The number of monkeys grew fast.	5
A politician decided to bring more monkeys in.	3
The monkeys received royal attention.	**4**
The monkeys arrived in Gibraltar.	2

Aufgabe 4

Hinweis: *Gehe die einzelnen Aussagen durch und vergleiche sie mit dem Text (inkl. der Grafik zum Skywalk). Sie sind in chronologischer Reihenfolge angeordnet, sodass du ungefähr weißt, wo du im Text suchen musst, um herauszufinden, ob eine Aussage stimmt.*

(1) c

Hinweis: *Z. 14f.*

(2) e

Hinweis: *Z. 17*

(3) i

Hinweis: *Grafik Seite 5: "resists wind speeds up to 150 km/h"*

D Sprachmittlung

Allgemeiner Hinweis: *Bei der Sprachmittlung kommt es darauf an, dass du – in diesem Fall – einem englischen Text wesentliche Aspekte entnimmst und auf Deutsch wiedergibst. Dabei musst du nicht direkt übersetzen. In der folgenden Aufgabe sind sowohl die Form („Beitrag für die Schülerzeitung") sowie vier Anweisungen, welche Punkte du in deinen Text aufnehmen sollst, vorgegeben. In der Beispiellösung sind diese Punkte für dich jeweils noch einmal in Klammern angegeben. Lies dir die Punkte in der Aufgabenstellung gut durch, damit du weißt, auf was du achten musst, und damit du nichts übersiehst, auf was du eingehen sollst.*

Beispiellösung:
(Ursprung der Legende:)
Ende des 18. Jahrhunderts unternahmen die Franzosen und Spanier einen Überraschungsangriff auf das von den Briten kontrollierte Gibraltar. Dieser Angriff löste unter den Affen Unruhe aus und sie machten großen Lärm. Dadurch waren die Briten gewarnt und konnten den Angriff abwehren.
(Verhalten der Affen im Kontakt mit Menschen:)
Die Affen können aggressiv sein und es kann passieren, dass sie Menschen auf den Rücken springen oder an ihnen hochklettern. Sie stehlen auch gerne Taschen oder Essen.
(Verhaltenstipps für Personen, die den Affenfelsen besuchen; davon zwei Aspekte:)
Man sollte sich möglichst auf offenen Flächen aufhalten, und wenn es eng wird (z. B. auf Treppen oder in einem Tunnel) etwas zurückweichen, um den Affen mehr Platz zu lassen. Auch sollte man nicht in die Hocke gehen. Wichtig ist, dass man die Affen nicht füttert, sonst droht eine hohe Geldstrafe.
(Folgen des Kontakts mit den Menschen für die Affen; davon zwei Aspekte:)

Das Füttern schädigt die Gesundheit der Affen und auch deren soziale Ordnung. Durch das Füttern werden sie außerdem abhängig von den Menschen.

E Text- und Medienkompetenzen

Hinweis: *Im Bereich „Text- und Medienkompetenzen" bekommst du einen Text auf Englisch vorgelegt, in diesem Fall eine Unterhaltung in einem Chat, in der es um einen Rucksack geht, der von einem Affen gestohlen wurde. Dabei musst du Informationen aus diesem Chat in ein anderes englisches Textformat übertragen, hier ein Suchplakat für den Rucksack. Es reichen dabei Stichpunkte. Beachte, dass die Reihenfolge, in der die Informationen in den Texten vorkommen, nicht unbedingt gleich ist. Bei 4–6 kannst du die Informationen in der Reihenfolge angeben, wie sie im Text vorkommen, aber du kannst sie auch beliebig anordnen.*

Beispiellösung:

(1) Backpack missing/gone/stolen /
Help! A monkey has stolen my backpack! /
Help needed!

(2) right after breakfast / in the morning

(3) middle station of the cable car

(4) black

(5) broken zip

(6) silver key ring with an "R" on it

(7) what / what's in it / what's inside it / content(s)

(8) hotel room key

(9) bank card

F Schreiben

Allgemeiner Hinweis: *Lies dir beide Aufgabenstellungen erst einmal gut durch und entscheide dich dann entweder für die E-Mail oder für die Bildergeschichte. Berücksichtige die Vorgaben, die in der Aufgabenstellung enthalten sind. Achte auf einen klaren Satzbau, abwechslungsreichen Wortschatz sowie die Rechtschreibung. Verwende das Wörterbuch, und prüfe immer wieder, ob dein Text sprachlich richtig und inhaltlich schlüssig und verständlich ist. Du erhältst sowohl für den Inhalt als auch für die sprachliche Gestaltung Punkte. Halte dich an den vorgeschriebenen Umfang, schreibe leserlich und achte auf eine saubere äußere Form. Die folgenden Texte sind Lösungsbeispiele.*

Correspondence: E-Mail

Hinweis: *In der Aufgabenstellung wird zunächst die Schreibsituation erklärt. Anschließend wird aufgezählt, welche Inhalte deine E-Mail enthalten muss. Dabei ist wichtig, dass du alle Vorgaben in deiner E-Mail umsetzt.*
Verfasse nun deinen Text. Deine E-Mail geht an Dani, deine spanische Austauschpartnerin, d. h., du kannst dich auch etwas umgangssprachlicher ausdrücken und z. B. Kurzformen verwenden (z. B. „I'm"). Versuche aber, in ganzen Sätzen zu schreiben und diese mit Konjunktionen (Bindewörtern) zu verbinden. Unbekannte Wörter kannst du im Wörterbuch nachschlagen.
Lies deine E-Mail am Ende noch einmal durch und überprüfe, ob dein Text leserlich und verständlich ist, ob er den geforderten Umfang hat und ob du alle Punkte in deinem Text übernommen hast. Hake auf dem Angabenblatt die Inhalte ab, die du übernommen hast. Eine genaue Anleitung zum Schreiben einer E-Mail findest du übrigens im Kompetenzbereich „Schreiben" im Trainingsteil des Aufgabenbandes.

Beispiellösung:

Dear Dani,

My name is Andrea and I'm looking forward to staying with you in Marbella. I'm 15 years old and I'm in class 9a at your partner school in Regensburg.
I'm curious to know what school is like in Spain. What are the school hours? Are there any special rules I should know?
Maybe you could tell me something about my stay with your family. Am I going to have my own room and do you have a good internet connection?
Perhaps you already have some ideas about what we could do in our free time – like going to some cool events, for example.
I also wanted to tell you that I'm a vegetarian, which I hope is OK for your family.
One final question: As Gibraltar is not too far away from Marbella, would it be possible to go there?

Take care and kind regards to your family!

Andrea *(151 words)*

Creative Writing: Picture story

Hinweis: *In der Aufgabenstellung werden dir die Überschrift und der Beginn der Geschichte vorgegeben. Schreibe sie ab und setze die Geschichte passend fort. Sieh dir die Bilder genau an – auch die Sprech- und Gedankenblasen, die dir Hinweise auf die Handlung geben und die du in deinen Text einbauen kannst.*

Verfasse nun deine Geschichte in der Vergangenheitsform „simple past" (Last Monday …). Schreibe in ganzen Sätzen und versuche, diese mit Konjunktionen (Bindewörtern) zu verbinden. Um die Geschichte auszuschmücken, kannst du z. B. die wörtliche Rede, Adjektive sowie Orts- und Zeitangaben verwenden. Überprüfe zum Schluss, ob deine Geschichte dem geforderten Umfang entspricht und auch dann verständlich ist, wenn man die Bilder nicht kennt. Eine genaue Anleitung zum Schreiben einer Bildergeschichte findest du im Kompetenzbereich „Schreiben" im Trainingsteil des Aufgabenbandes. Der folgende Text ist eine Beispiellösung.

Happy Ending

Last Monday morning, during the first lesson, Keith had trouble concentrating, because his seat was right behind Nicole's, with whom he was so in love. He was staring at the back of her head and her beautiful dark hair, while Nicole was busily doing the test.

After the lesson, when he was walking down the hallway, Keith saw Nicole and her friend standing in front of a poster which said that there were tickets for *Swan Lake* on sale, and he heard Nicole telling her friend that she was happy she had got a ticket for the ballet. Suddenly Keith had an idea!

He went to the box office immediately and bought a ticket for *Swan Lake* too.

On the night of the ballet, Keith was very lucky to sit only a few seats away from Nicole. When she saw Keith, she was surprised but also happy to see him.

During the break, they met in the foyer and talked a lot – and not only about the ballet …

A few days later, Keith swapped seats with a classmate so that he could sit right next to Nicole and hold hands with her. Nicole liked that, too …

(191 words)

Notenschlüssel

Notenstufen	1	2	3	4	5	6
Punkte	92–78	77,5–63	62,5–47	46,5–31	30,5–16	15,5–0

Qualifizierender Abschluss der Mittelschule Bayern 2017
Lösungen – Englisch

A Listening Comprehension

Allgemeiner Hinweis: *In diesem Teil der Prüfung musst du Hörtexten Informationen entnehmen. Du hörst zuerst einen Dialog, in dem es um die Suche nach einem Ausbildungsplatz geht. Im zweiten Hörtext wird von einer Arbeitserfahrung in Australien berichtet. Der dritte Text ist ein Bewerbungsgespräch. Im vierten Hörtext folgst du einem Kundengespräch in einer Autowerkstatt.*
Jeder Hörtext wird zweimal vorgespielt. Du hast in den Pausen vor und nach den Texten ausreichend Zeit, um die Aufgabenstellungen durchzulesen bzw. die Lösungen einzutragen.

Aufgabe 1

Kim: Hello?

Uncle Bob: Hi, Kim. It's your uncle Bob. How are you getting on? Are you still looking for a job as a car mechanic?

Kim: Yes, no luck so far, I'm afraid.

Uncle Bob: Well, I've just seen an advert in the local newspaper. Brown's Garage is offering an apprenticeship. Are you interested?

Kim: Hmm … what qualifications are required?

Uncle Bob: Let me see … You have to be at least 16 years old … They want good grades in maths and physics … It also says that some work experience would be helpful, but it's not absolutely necessary. And you don't need a driving licence.

Kim: Aha, OK. And do you know where Brown's Garage is?

Uncle Bob: Yes, it's not far from my house.

Kim: Oh, so it's in Brighton? And you know them?

Uncle Bob: Yes, I've been taking my car there for years. They are very reliable, and friendly, too.

Kim: Oh, and how can I get in touch with them?

Uncle Bob: I suggest you contact David, he is the head mechanic. He will be able to give you more information about the job. He is an interesting guy. He used to work in Australia as a car mechanic for a while. He even has his own video blog. I'll find the link and send it to you.

Kim: Thanks, uncle Bob.

Uncle Bob: That's OK, bye.

Hinweis: *Da die Reihenfolge der Teilaufgaben der Abfolge im Hörtext entspricht, kannst du die fehlenden Informationen der Reihe nach dem Gespräch entnehmen. Achte vor allem bei Aufgabe 5 auf die richtige Schreibung. Wenn du hier anstatt „head mechanic" „hat mechanic" schreibst, wird aus der richtigen Lösung „Kfz-Meister" (sozusagen der „Chef-Mechaniker") ein „Hut-Mechaniker", was natürlich keinen Sinn ergibt.*

1. Kim could do an apprenticeship at **Brown's** Garage.
   Hinweis: *Z. 5 f.*
2. Kim must have good grades in **maths** and **physics**.
   Hinweis: *Z. 8 f.*
3. Kim doesn't need work experience or a **driving licence/driver's license/driver's licence**.
   Hinweis: *Z. 9 f.*
4. The garage is in **Brighton**.
   Hinweis: *Z. 13 f.*
5. David, the **head** mechanic, has more information about the job.
   Hinweis: *Z. 17 f.; die Lösungen „hat" und „had" sind falsch.*

Aufgabe 2

DAVID MCKINLEY: Hi everyone. My name is David McKinley. I'm from Brighton and I'm a car mechanic.

I worked for a while in Australia as a mobile mechanic. People over there often live so far away that they don't have the time to take their car to the garage. They want repairs on the spot.

I had a truck with all my tools in it and I went where the work was. That was anything … from doing a safety check in town to changing tyres on a van or fixing the brakes of a road train way out in the country.

If I didn't have the parts I needed, I had to use what I had in the truck. I spent whole nights working under broken-down trucks and more than once I was up to my knees in water trying to pull a jeep out of a swamp.

People were always pleased to see me but in some cases I couldn't repair their vehicles. So I ended up towing them for miles to the next town.

Did I like working there? Yes, sure. You just had to remember that there were snakes and spiders everywhere, even in your car! Lots of variety, lots of surprises. But I met all kinds of people and made some friends for life.

If you want to know more please feel free to contact me …

Hinweis: *Du findest hier eine Auflistung verschiedener Aussagen. Wähle die vier Aussagen aus, die sinngemäß im Hörtext vorkommen. Es ist egal, in welcher Reihenfolge du sie notierst.*

1. **Hinweis:** *D – „repairs on the spot“ (Z. 4 f.)*
2. **Hinweis:** *F – „whole nights“ (Z. 9 f.)*
3. **Hinweis:** *G – „up to my knees in water“ (Z. 10 f.)*
4. **Hinweis:** *I – „remember that there were snakes and spiders“ (Z. 14 f.)*

1	2	3	4
D	F	G	I

Aufgabe 3

MR BROWN: Good afternoon, Kim. I am Mr Brown, the manager.

KIM: Hello.

MR BROWN: So, you are interested in the job as a car mechanic. Tell me something about yourself.

KIM: Well, I'm sixteen years old and I'll finish school this summer. My favourite subject is maths and I am also very good at science. In my free time I play field hockey and I also like go-kart racing.

MR BROWN: Why do you want to be a car mechanic? It's not a typical job for girls, is it?

KIM: Everyone keeps telling me that. But I have always been interested in cars. For years, now, I've been helping my dad repair our family car. I did my work experience at our local garage. I'm good at working with my hands and I don't mind getting them dirty.

MR BROWN: Well, that sounds promising. Do you think you are strong enough to do the job?

KIM: Oh, I noticed when I worked in the garage that modern tools do most of the heavy work for you.

MR BROWN: I see. Well, do you have any questions about the job?

KIM: Hmm … yes. What are the working hours?

MR BROWN: We work from 8 am till 5 pm Mondays to Fridays with an hour's break for lunch. You have three weeks' holiday a year. At the beginning you will get £ 125 a week, but your salary will be a little higher next year. When would you be able to start?

KIM: The first of September, if that is all right with you.

Mr Brown: Oh yes, that would be perfect. I will need to have a closer look at your application and references. I'll let you know my decision by Monday. Is that OK?

Kim: Yes, thank you Mr Brown.

Mr Brown: Well, Kim … thank you very much for coming along. Goodbye.

Kim: Goodbye.

Mr Brown: Perhaps we'll see each other again in September …

Hinweis: *Beantworte die Fragen in Stichpunkten (Wort- oder Ziffernangabe). Achte auf die Fragewörter.*

1. this summer/in the summer
   Hinweis: *siehe Z. 5; when? (= wann?)*
2. (her) dad/father
   Hinweis: *siehe Z. 11; who? (= wer?)*
3. modern tools
   Hinweis: *siehe Z. 16 f.; what? (= was?)*
4. (£) 125 (a) week
   Hinweis: *siehe Z. 22; how much? (= wie viel?)*
5. 1 (st) September/September 1 (st)/the first of September
   Hinweis: *siehe Z. 24; when?*
6. Monday
   Hinweis: *siehe Z. 26; when?*

Aufgabe 4

Kim: Good morning, how can I help you?

Customer: Good morning. My car is making a strange noise. Could you have a look at it?

Kim: Yes, but not until this afternoon. Can you leave your car here?

Customer: Oh, no, I definitely need my car. Can't you take a look at it now?

Kim: Hmm, … we're rather busy this morning. Er, Dave! Could you help us a moment?

David: Yes? Good morning. As Kim said, we're rather busy. If you leave your car here, we can let you have a rental car. It's only £ 27.50 per day, including 200 miles and insurance.

Customer: Er, … is it like my car?

David: Well, in fact it's the same car, just an older model but with automatic and air conditioning.

Customer: And what about the fuel?

DAVID: We prefer you to return the car full. Otherwise we charge an extra £ 50. It's a diesel, by the way. We'll contact you as soon as we know what is wrong with your car. Could you leave your phone number with us?

CUSTOMER: Yes, of course. But ... please don't call before 2 pm.

DAVID: That's fine. Now you only need to show me your driver's license and your credit card ...

Hinweis: *Hier musst du die fehlenden Angaben in ein Formular eintragen.*

1. 27.50
   Hinweis: *Z. 9*
2. air conditioning
   Hinweis: *Z. 13*
3. diesel
   Hinweis: *Z. 15 f.*
4. 50
   Hinweis: *Z. 15*
5. 2 pm
   Hinweis: *Z. 18*

B Use of English

Allgemeiner Hinweis: *In diesem Prüfungsteil werden deine Wortschatz- und Grammatikkenntnisse getestet. Als Aufgabenform liegen dir Texte vor, in denen fehlende Wörter ergänzt oder sprachliche Fehler verbessert werden müssen. Dieser Aufgabentyp ist anspruchsvoll, da gleichzeitig Wortschatz, Grammatik und Rechtschreibung überprüft werden und die Inhalte nicht eingegrenzt sind (z. B. auf ein spezielles Grammatikthema).*

Aufgabe 1

Hinweis: *Lies dir zunächst den Lückentext durch und versuche, den Inhalt grob zu verstehen. Anschließend gehst du die E-Mail erneut durch, diesmal Satz für Satz. Überlege dabei, welches Wort im Satzzusammenhang einen Sinn ergibt. Muss dieses Wort noch (z. B. durch Verwendung einer bestimmten Zeitform) in den Satz eingepasst werden?*

(1) „for" gibt einen Zeitraum an (hier: „für die nächsten zwei Wochen")
(2) „if/whether" = „ob"; ebenfalls möglich: „and"
(3) „than" → Steigerung/Vergleich (hier: „mehr als ...")

(4) *„works/is" (Simple present); „worked/was" (Simple past) ist ebenfalls möglich, wenn ausgedrückt werden soll, dass der Gastvater früher einmal in der Firma gearbeitet hat*
(5) *„has ... improved" (Present perfect) → Seit („since") Martin in England ist, hat sich sein Englisch schon verbessert (etwas hat also in der Vergangenheit begonnen und wirkt sich auf die Gegenwart aus).*
(6) *„will ... recommend" (Will-future) → „When I'm back home" zeigt ein zukünftiges Ereignis an; im Hauptsatz muss dann das Will-future stehen.*
(7) *„looking forward to hearing" → feststehende Redewendung mit -ing-Form („sich freuen auf")*

Hello Julia,

How are you? I (0) **am** writing to you from Birmingham. I'll be here (1) **for** the next two weeks. My company asked me (2) **if/whether/and** I was interested in working in Britain this summer. As you can imagine, I was more (3) **than** happy. I'm staying with a very nice family and the host father (4) **works/worked/is/was** in the same factory. I am the only German here so I have to talk English all the time. I think my English (5) **has** already improved quite a lot since I arrived here. I am really enjoying my stay and I love working here.
When I'm back home I (6) **will** definitely recommend such a visit to my colleagues. I am looking forward to (7) **hearing** from you soon.

Love,
Martin

Aufgabe 2

Hinweis: *Hier musst du aus den Wörtern im Kasten das jeweils passende Wort für die Lücken im Text auswählen. Es stehen dabei mehr Wörter zur Auswahl, als du brauchst. Überlege zunächst, welches Wort du in deiner Muttersprache auswählen würdest. Finde dann das richtige englische Wort und füge es ein.*
(1) *abroad (= im Ausland)*
(2) *because of (= wegen)*
(3) *while (= während)*
(4) *could spend time (= könnten Zeit verbringen)*
(5) *<u>at</u> my aunt's = (<u>bei</u> meiner Tante)*
(6) *in <u>that</u> area (= in <u>dieser</u> Gegend)*
(7) *think about (= hier: halten von)*

Dear Martin,

What a pleasant surprise (0) **having** you here in Britain. Did all the trainees have the chance to work (1) **abroad** or did your company choose you (2) **because** of your excellent results in your exams? You have to tell me more about it.
I would love to see you (3) **while** you are here. I could come to Birmingham next weekend so that we could (4) **spend** some time together. I could stay (5) **at** my aunt's. Have I ever mentioned that my mum's sister and her family live in (6) **that** area? My cousin Jo told me about an amusement park which is interesting and not far away. What do you think (7) **about** spending a day there? Perhaps together with Jo? If you like my idea or if you have any other suggestions, please write back soon, so we can fix a date.

Love,
Julia

Aufgabe 3

Hinweis: *Hier sollst du in einem Brief sechs Grammatikfehler finden, die du auch verbessern musst. An den Linien in der rechten Spalte, auf die du die richtigen Wörter schreiben sollst, erkennst du leicht, in welcher Zeile sich ein Fehler befindet. Die Fehler lassen sich meist aus dem Satzzusammenhang erklären.*
In der folgenden Lösung findest du den Brief mit den unterstrichenen Fehlern. Danach folgen die richtigen Wörter (1–6) mit Hinweisen.

Dear all,

I arrived home safely after a pleasant flight, although the departure was delayed for **0.** much than one hour. Unfortunately, my suitcase was not on the plane, but **1.** he was delivered to my house by the airline later. So I was able to give the presents to my family. My grandma **2.** love the teapot and especially the tea.
My brother immediately put on the football shirt of the English national team and **3.** doesn't want to take it off again until he went to bed. My father and my sister liked **4.** her gifts, too.
I am so grateful that you helped me to find souvenirs for everybody. My visit went by very quickly and I've already **5.** be back at work **6.** since five days, but I have so many pleasant memories of my stay in England.
Best regards and thanks from my parents.

Love,
Martin

0. more
   Hinweis: *more than = mehr als (Steigerung)*
1. it
   Hinweis: *suitcase → it*
2. loves/loved
   Hinweis: *my grandma (= she) = 3. Person Singular → loves (Simple present); oder: loved (Simple past)*
3. didn't/did not
   Hinweis: *went to bed (Simple past) → gleiche Zeit verwenden: didn't/did not*
4. their
   Hinweis: *father and sister = 3. Person Plural → their (Possessivpronomen)*
5. been
   Hinweis: *I've been (Present perfect)*
6. for
   Hinweis: *five days = Zeitraum → for*

C Reading Comprehension

Allgemeiner Hinweis: *In diesem Prüfungsteil stellst du dein Leseverstehen unter Beweis, indem du Aufgaben zum Grob- und Detailverständnis bearbeitest. Beim ersten Durchlesen gewinnst du einen Überblick, worum es im Text geht. Wenn du den Text ein zweites Mal liest, konzentriere dich darauf, ihn möglichst genau zu verstehen. Dann beginnst du mit dem dazugehörigen Aufgabenteil. Suche diejenigen Abschnitte oder Stellen im Text heraus, auf die sich die Aufgabe bezieht. Oft kannst du Satzteile, Angaben oder Wörter direkt aus dem Text als Antwort übernehmen und auf diese Weise z. B. Rechtschreibfehler vermeiden.*

Vokabelhinweise:
Du findest nachfolgend eine Liste mit schwierigen Vokabeln aus dem Text. Zur Vorbereitung auf die Prüfung solltest du aber versuchen, möglichst viele Wörter aus dem Zusammenhang zu erschließen, sowie den Umgang mit dem Wörterbuch einzuüben. Aus Zeitgründen kannst du in der schriftlichen Prüfung nur die Wörter nachschlagen, die du unbedingt zum Verständnis benötigst.

Z. 1: entertainment: Unterhaltung
Z. 3: funfair: Jahrmarkt
Z. 5: influence: Einfluss
Z. 15: to include: enthalten, etwas aufnehmen
Z. 17: educational purpose: Bildungs-/erzieherischer Zweck
Z. 23: enclosed: hier: überdacht, sich im Innern befindend
Z. 24: Ferris wheel: Riesenrad
Z. 24: common: hier: verbreitet

Z. 27: admission fee: Eintrittspreis
Z. 30: to charge: berechnen
Z. 30 f.: to be entitled: berechtigt sein
Z. 32: beverage: Getränk
Z. 34: latest technology: modernste/ neueste Technik
Z. 37: added: hier: hinzugefügt
Z. 42: recreational activities: Freizeitaktivitäten
Z. 43: misbehavior: Fehlverhalten
Z. 44: restriction: Beschränkung
Z. 46: restraints: hier: Sicherheitsvorrichtungen (Gurte, Bügel)
Z. 47: harness: hier: Gurt
Z. 47: lap bar: Bügel über dem Schoß
Z. 47: handrail: Handlauf, Geländer
Z. 49: belongings: hier: persönliche Dinge
Z. 51: temporary: vorübergehend
Z. 53: maintained: gewartet

Aufgabe 1

Hinweis: *Ordne jedem Absatz (paragraph) die inhaltlich passende Überschrift zu.*

Vokabelhinweise:
development: Entwicklung; accommodation: Unterkunft

paragraph B	paragraph C	paragraph D	paragraph E	paragraph F
2	**6**	**7**	**3**	**4**

Aufgabe 2

Hinweis: *Hier musst du die Fragen mit Informationen aus dem Text beantworten. Dabei sind Kurzantworten möglich.*
Fragewörter (z. B. who) und Schlüsselwörter (z. B. pleasure gardens – „Lustgärten", model – „Vorbild", device – „Gerät, Apparat") geben dir einen Hinweis, nach welcher Information du im Text suchen musst.

1. rich people
   Hinweis: *Z. 9*
2. (the) Prater (in Vienna)
   Hinweis: *Z. 10 ff.*
3. dark rides/ghost trains
   Hinweis: *Z. 23*
4. pay-one-price (scheme)
   Hinweis: *Z. 30*
5. (mobile) virtual reality headsets/headsets that present 3D adventures
   Hinweis: *Z. 37*

Aufgabe 3

Hinweis: *Bei dieser Aufgabe sind – ähnlich wie im Wörterbuch – verschiedene Wortbedeutungen vorgegeben. Die deutsche Bedeutung hängt davon ab, welche Funktion das Wort im Satz hat (z. B. Nomen – Namenwort, Verb – Tunwort, Adjektiv – Wiewort) und in welchem Sinnzusammenhang es im Text verwendet wird. Mithilfe der Zeilenangabe findest du das gesuchte Wort im Text. Lies und übersetze nun diesen Satz(teil), indem du jeweils eine der angegebenen Möglichkeiten verwendest. So kannst du die richtige Übersetzung herausfinden.*

1. focus (line 17)
   - ☐ Mittelpunkt *(Nomen)*
   - ☐ klar sehen *(Verb)*
   - ☐ Brennpunkt *(Nomen)*
   - ☑ sich konzentrieren *(Verb)*

   Hinweis: *Einige Parks konzentrieren sich auf urzeitliche Tiere, ...*

2. drop (line 21)
   - ☐ tropfen *(Verb)*
   - ☐ Tropfen *(Nomen)*
   - ☑ Fall *(Nomen)*
   - ☐ fallen lassen *(Verb)*

   Hinweis: *Klassische Fahrgeschäfte sind die Achterbahnen, bei denen für gewöhnlich ein tiefer Fall vom höchsten Punkt aus dazugehört, ...*

3. mobile (line 37)
   - ☐ Handy *(Nomen)*
   - ☑ transportabel *(Adj.)*
   - ☐ Mobile *(Nomen)*
   - ☐ flexibel *(Adj.)*

   Hinweis: *Fahrgäste tragen transportable Headsets, die eine virtuelle Realität erzeugen ...*

4. fit (line 46)
   - ☑ passen *(Verb)*
   - ☐ geeignet *(Adj.)*

- [ ] Anfall *(Nomen)*
- [ ] in Form *(Adj.)*

Hinweis: *Achte darauf, dass die Sicherheitsvorrichtungen gut passen, …*

5. board (line 53)
   - [ ] Brett *(Nomen)*
   - [ ] Behörde *(Nomen)*
   - [x] einsteigen *(Verb)*
   - [ ] verschlafen *(Verb)*

   Hinweis: *Steige nicht in ein Fahrgeschäft ein, wenn es schlecht gewartet aussieht, …*

Aufgabe 4

Hinweis: *Wähle aus den Aussagen (b–j) diejenigen fünf, die dem Lesetext inhaltlich entsprechen. Die Aussagen sind in derselben Reihenfolge angeordnet wie die zugehörigen Informationen im Lesetext. Um die richtigen Aussagen auszuwählen, musst du die Aussagen und den Lesetext genau verstanden haben. Lies die entsprechenden Textteile sorgfältig durch und schlage unbekannte Vokabeln im Wörterbuch nach. Beachte, dass die Aussagen im Text oft anders formuliert sind, aber (bei der richtigen Lösung) inhaltlich übereinstimmen.*
Beispiel:
Aussage: a) Usually amusement parks are very large.
Text: Z. 1 f.: „Amusement park … in a large outdoor area, often covering many square kilometers."

1. d

   Hinweis: *„animals, fish and other sea life" (Z. 18 f.) = „creatures of the ocean"*
2. f

   Hinweis: *„transport rides" (Z. 25 f.) = „easy way to get around"*
3. h

   Hinweis: *„Considering the speed with which society and technology are changing … expect a lot of new attractions …" (Z. 39 f.) = „Fast developing technology … many possibilities for future park attractions"*
4. i

   Hinweis: *„age … restrictions" (Z. 44) = „old enough"*
5. j

   Hinweis: *„stay seated" (Z. 51) = „Don't get off …"*

D Text Production

Allgemeiner Hinweis: *Lies dir beide Aufgabenstellungen erst einmal sorgfältig durch. Entscheide dich dann entweder für den Brief (Bewerbungsschreiben/Lebenslauf) oder für die Bildergeschichte. Berücksichtige die Vorgaben, die in der Aufgabenstellung enthalten sind. Achte auf einen klaren Satzbau, abwechslungsreichen Wortschatz, sowie die Rechtschreibung. Verwende das Wörterbuch, und kontrolliere immer wieder, ob dein Text sprachlich und inhaltlich schlüssig und verständlich ist. Du erhältst Punkte sowohl auf den Inhalt als auch auf die sprachliche Gestaltung. Halte dich an den vorgeschriebenen Umfang, schreibe leserlich und achte auf eine saubere äußere Form. Die folgenden Texte sind Lösungsbeispiele.*

Correspondence: Application and CV

Hinweis: *Diese Schreibaufgabe besteht aus einem Anschreiben (Höchstpunktzahl: 16 P.) und einem tabellarischen Lebenslauf (Höchstpunktzahl: 4 P.). Das Anschreiben verfasst du als formellen Brief, in dem du die Vorgaben der Aufgabenstellung unterbringst. Wähle außerdem eine passende Anrede (Ansprechpartner: Herr Johnson), und vergiss die Grußformel sowie deinen Namen nicht. Der Lebenslauf wird in Form einer Tabelle verfasst. Bei den Gliederungspunkten gibst du stichpunktartig Auskunft über deine Person, deine Schulbildung und weitere Aspekte. Deine Angaben können auch erfunden sein, solange sie glaubhaft wirken.*

6 November 20...

Dear Mr Johnson,

I am writing to you with regard to the holiday jobs in an amusement park which I found on your agency's website. I am interested in any type of work that includes direct contact with the park's visitors, for example explaining an attraction to them or helping them to use it.
I would like to have a holiday job in England because it would help me to improve my English. This is really important to me because I want to be a travel agent after school. I already have some work experience. Our church organised a camping trip for children last year, and I helped to take care of a group of seven girls for four days. I really liked the job.
I would have time to work in the amusement park in my Easter holidays next year (24 March–8 April). Is it possible to have accommodation in the park, and is there a canteen for the employees?
I have included my CV, and look forward to hearing from you.

Yours sincerely,
Charlotte Müller *(185 words)*

Curriculum Vitae

Personal information	Charlotte Müller, Regnitzwall 7, 90760 Fürth Phone: +49-911/0102030 Age: 15
Education	Elementary school: Grundschule Herrenstraße, Fürth Middle school: Franken-Mittelschule, Fürth
Practical experience	Took care of 7 children during church camping trip Delivery of newspapers twice a week
Special knowledge	Good in English Computer skills
Personal interests	Nature, dogs, travel (England & France)

(54 words)

Creative Writing: Picture and Prompts

Hinweis: *Hier musst du eine Geschichte (und keine Bildbeschreibung!) auf Englisch verfassen. Als Impulse für deine Geschichte liegen dir ein Bild sowie Stichwörter vor. Die Stichwörter verdeutlichen die Handlung oder geben dir Anregungen, wie du deinen Text ausgestalten kannst. An welcher Stelle in deiner Geschichte du diese Vorgaben einbringen willst, entscheidest du selbst. Die Überschrift sowie der Anfang der Geschichte sind vorgegeben. Anhand des Einleitungssatzes („Last year …") erkennst du auch, dass als Zeitform hauptsächlich das Simple past zu verwenden ist. Teile deine Geschichte in Einleitung, Hauptteil und Schluss ein. Der Umfang sollte mindestens 100 Wörter betragen. Achte darauf, dass dein Text vollständig, nachvollziehbar und gut lesbar ist. Du erhältst sowohl Punkte auf den Inhalt als auch auf die sprachliche Ausgestaltung (z. B. Wortwahl, Satzbau, Rechtschreibung).*

What a shock!

Last year Barbara took her English friend Megan to the Oktoberfest. Megan was very excited because Barbara's sister had lent her a dirndl dress. She was so happy to be wearing it that she could not stop taking pictures of Barbara and herself. When Megan saw a carousel she exclaimed: "This classic old ride would go so well with my dirndl in a photo", and bought two tickets. When the two girls were spinning around, Megan yelled, "Wow, this is great! I'm going to make a video of the two of us!" Barbara shouted back, "Cool, but don't lose your phone!", but it was already too late. The phone had slipped from Megan's hand, and fell straight onto the hat of a man wearing lederhosen. The man's wife saw the phone falling down and cried out: "Oh no, watch out!"

When the merry-go-round turned again to where the man and the woman were standing, Barbara and Megan saw that the man was holding his hat and the phone in his hands. He looked up in their direction and waved. Barbara and Megan waved back. When the ride was over, the girls went to the man. “I’m so sorry,” Megan apologised. The woman was angry and wanted to shout at them, but the man just smiled and gave Megan her phone. Megan invited the couple to a “Maß” of beer. Then she took a selfie of the four of them as a special souvenir. *(244 words)*

Notenschlüssel

Notenstufen	1	2	3	4	5	6
Punkte	80–68	67–55	54–41	40–27	26–13	12–0

Qualifizierender Abschluss der Mittelschule Bayern 2018
Lösungen – Englisch

A Listening Comprehension

Allgemeiner Hinweis: *Jeder Hörtext wird zweimal vorgespielt. Du hast in den Pausen vor und nach den Texten ausreichend Zeit, um die Aufgabenstellungen durchzulesen bzw. die Lösungen einzutragen.*

Aufgabe 1

Lauren: Hi Toby. What are your plans for the weekend?

Toby: Well, I'm going rock-climbing in the Rocky Mountains on Saturday. But I'm free on Sunday.

Lauren: Great! What about going to the zoo?

Toby: The zoo, … hmm. I don't know. I haven't been there since I was 10.

Lauren: Well, then it's certainly time for another visit! I love Calgary Zoo. I go there almost every month. I've even got a season ticket. It's only 60 Canadian dollars and you can go as often as you like for a whole year. My younger brother loves it, too. His favorite animals are the crocodiles and the dinosaurs.

Toby: Dinosaurs?

Lauren: Yeah, well, one part of the zoo is called the *Prehistoric Park*. There are models of dinosaurs, more than 20 of them. The biggest are almost 30 metres long. The *Prehistoric Park* has just reopened though. It had been closed for seven months because of repair work. Some of the models were damaged by that horrible storm last October. They have also put up some new ones. It's one of the best parts of the zoo, especially when the weather is nice.

Toby: But what if it rains?

Lauren: Oh, I've already listened to the weather forecast for this weekend. It'll be windy and cool on Saturday. But on Sunday, the weather will be perfect for a visit to the zoo. It'll be sunny and warm, with temperatures above 25 degrees.

Toby: Wow, sounds great. Let's go then.

Lauren: Well, when and where shall we meet?

Toby: What about 9.30?

Lauren: The zoo doesn't open until 10 on Sundays. Let's meet at 10.30 at the zoo entrance.

Hinweis: *In jedem Satz (1–8) unterscheidet sich ein Wort vom Hörtext. Streiche das falsche Wort im Satz durch und notiere das richtige Wort aus dem Hörtext. Da manche Wörter recht ähnlich klingen, solltest du genau zuhören.*

1. I haven't been there since I was **10/ten**.
   Hinweis: *Z. 5*
2. I've even got a **season** ticket.
   Hinweis: *Z. 7*
3. It's only **60/sixty** Canadian dollars and you can go as often as you like.
   Hinweis: *Z. 7 f.*
4. My younger brother's favorite animals are the crocodiles and the **dinosaurs**.
   Hinweis: *Z. 9*
5. It had been closed for seven **months** because of repair work.
   Hinweis: *Z. 13 f.*
6. Some of the models were damaged by that horrible **storm** last October.
   Hinweis: *Z. 14 f.*
7. It'll be windy and **cool** on Saturday.
   Hinweis: *Z. 18 f.*
8. The zoo doesn't open **until / till** 10 on Sundays.
   Hinweis: *Z. 24*

Aufgabe 2

Lauren: Hello?

Toby: Hi, it's me.

Lauren: Toby, I'm waiting for you. You're already 10 minutes late! Where are you?

Toby: I'm sorry. I'm still in the city centre. I don't know how to get to the zoo.

Lauren: What's the problem? Just take the C-train. It's line 202. You should know that.

Toby: I know that, but there are no trains between 4th Street and City Hall on line 202 because of construction work. The service is going to reopen at 11 o'clock.

Lauren: 11 o'clock! But that means it will be almost 11.30 when you arrive here. Isn't there any quicker way?

Toby: Not a chance.

Lauren: OK, but what am I going to do until you get here?

Toby: Why don't you go in? You don't have to stand around and wait for me. I know you want to see the penguins and the gorillas. I'm not really interested in them anyway, so you can go there on your own. But don't go to the grizzly bears without me. They're my favorite animals.

Lauren: All right then. Call me when you're at the entrance. I'll come and meet you there.

Toby: There's no need for that. Let's meet on the bridge across the river. It's in the middle of the zoo. That way you won't have to walk all the way back to the entrance.

Lauren: That sounds good. See you later.

Toby: See you later. Sorry again.

Hinweis: *Bei dieser Aufgabe ergänzt du mithilfe des Hörtextes fehlende Informationen. Sieh dir die unvollständigen Sätze (1–5) zunächst an. Obwohl diese Sätze nicht wortwörtlich im Hörtext vorkommen, enthalten sie dennoch Schlüsselwörter (z. B. „C-train", „favorite animals"), die auch im Hörtext vorkommen, und dir signalisieren, jetzt genau zuzuhören.*

Vokabelhinweis:
construction work (Z. 8): Bauarbeiten

1. Toby has to take the C-train, line **202**.
   Hinweis: *Z. 5*
2. At the moment, there are no trains because of **construction work**.
   Hinweis: *Z. 7 f.*
3. Toby will be at the zoo at about **11.30**.
   Hinweis: *Z. 9*
4. Toby's favorite animals are the **grizzly bears/grizzlies**.
   Hinweis: *Z. 15 f.*
5. They meet on the **bridge (across the river)** in the middle of the zoo.
   Hinweis: *Z. 19 f.*

Aufgabe 3

Zookeeper: Welcome everybody, my name is Dave and I'm here to tell you a little bit about Maska the grizzly bear, one of the stars of Calgary Zoo. His name is native American and means "strong". Maska is quite heavy, even for a male grizzly, which normally reaches about 380 kg; Maska weighs almost 450. When standing on his back legs, he is more than 2 metres tall. He's also faster than you might think. He can reach a speed of 60 kilometres per hour. He could easily catch Usain Bolt.

Maska has been at Calgary Zoo for 8 years now. We don't know Maska's exact age because he was born in the wilderness. He had to be captured because he was causing problems. Wild grizzlies usually stay away from humans. But Maska was often seen near villages and even in people's gardens looking for food in trashcans. He became a risk for the people living there. Some of them wanted to kill Maska. But before that happened, Maska was brought to our zoo. Our visitors think he's great, especially the children. They love it when he plays with the red ball over there, his favorite toy, although most of the time he's quite lazy. He enjoys resting in the sun.

Maska likes all kinds of food, like all grizzlies. So, on most days, we feed him a mix of apples, oranges, carrots and nuts. He also likes fish. Of course, he gets meat, too, but only once a week. The food he loves the most is hard-boiled eggs, but we only give him these on special occasions.

If you would like to watch him enjoying his meal, please come back in the afternoon …

Hinweis: *Diese Aufgabe erfordert hohe Konzentration, da du im Hörtext mit einer Vielzahl von Informationen (z. B. Namen, Daten) konfrontierst wirst. Du sollst aber nur genau die Wörter herausfiltern, die in Maskas Steckbrief fehlen. Orientiere dich deshalb an den Schlüsselwörtern in der Tabelle, da sie deine Aufmerksamkeit beim Hören auf die entscheidenden Stellen lenken.*

Vokabelhinweis:

Usain Bolt (Z. 7): ehemaliger Sprinter, mehrfacher Olympiasieger und Weltmeister;
he had to be captured (Z. 9): er musste eingefangen werden;
occasion (Z. 20): Gelegenheit, Anlass

1. (almost) 450
   Hinweis: *Z. 4*
2. 60/sixty
   Hinweis: *Z. 6*
3. villages, (people's) gardens
   Hinweis: *Z. 11*
4. food (in trashcans)
   Hinweis: *Z. 11 f.*
5. resting (in the sun)/being lazy
   Hinweis: *Z. 15 f.*

6. carrots
   Hinweis: *Z. 18*
7. once a week
   Hinweis: *Z. 19*

B Use of English

Allgemeiner Hinweis: *Du findest in diesem Prüfungsteil Aufgaben, in denen sprachliche Fehler verbessert oder Lückentexte ergänzt werden sollen. Diese Aufgabentypen sind anspruchsvoll, da gleichzeitig ein umfangreicher Wortschatz, sichere Rechtschreibung sowie gute Kenntnisse in unterschiedlichen Grammatikbereichen benötigt werden. Beachte, dass du dabei kein Wörterbuch verwenden darfst! Auch darfst du den vorgegebenen Text nicht verändern, indem du z. B. eine ganze Zeile streichst oder neue Satzteile hinzufügst.*

Aufgabe 1

Hinweis: *Lies den Text zur Geschichte der Eisenbahn in Kanada zunächst einmal als Ganzes durch. Vielleicht „stolperst" du dabei bereits über Wörter, die im Textzusammenhang sprachlich falsch sind. Suche danach gezielt nach den Fehlern. Die Zeilen (1–7) im Kasten rechts zeigen dir an, in welcher Textzeile sich ein Fehler befindet. Korrigiere den Fehler, indem du das das richtige Wort neben die Nummerierung auf die jeweilige Zeile schreibst. Solltest du bei dieser Aufgabe Schwierigkeiten haben, kann es dir helfen, die Grammatikbereiche im Buch (ab Seite 69) zu wiederholen.*

1. *more or less: mehr oder weniger; auch möglich: more and more: immer mehr*
2. *cheaper than: billiger als → Steigerung*
3. *by train: mit dem Zug*
4. *take the train: einen Zug nehmen*
5. *in/during the first half of the last century: in/während der 1. Hälfte des letzten Jahrhunderts*
6. *children who/that …: Kinder, die … → Relativpronomen; das Relativpronomen „which" wird nur für Sachen verwendet*
7. *were able to: konnten → Plural, da sich das Verb auf die Kinder bezieht*

In the early years the railway played a very important role in the development **0.** of Canada. Nowadays it is more **1.** or less / **1.** and more used to transport goods. Bus tickets are cheaper **2.** than train tickets and planes are more popular if you are short of time. But when you take the time and travel **3.** by train, the experience of traveling will certainly be unforgettable. Lots of tourists **4.** take the train through the Rocky Mountains and enjoy the incredible views of the landscape. Over the years the train has served many purposes. **5.** In/During the first half of the last century there used to be a wagon equipped with a classroom, a library and accommodation for a teacher. It traveled around the country every month and children **6.** who/that lived in remote areas **7.** were able to have at least two or three days' teaching each month before the train took the wagon to the next remote location.

Aufgabe 2

Hinweis: *Lies den Text erst einmal ganz durch, um den Inhalt grob zu erfassen. So fällt es dir leichter, die richtige Form der vorgegebenen Wörter zu finden. Achte dabei auf Signalwörter (z. B. „since") oder darauf, welche Funktion das Wort im Satz hat (z. B. Adjektiv, Adverb). Solltest du bei dieser Aufgabe Schwierigkeiten haben, kann es dir helfen, in der Kurzgrammatik (ab Seite 69) nachzusehen.*

1. *well-known: bekannt/berühmt*
2. *have been: Present perfect (Signalwort „since": „seit")*
3. *it offers: 3. Person Singular – das „s" muss mit!*
4. *to get close to sb/sth: jmd/etw nahekommen*
5. *easily: Adverb*
6. *to be included: „inbegriffen sein": Passiv*
7. *will not/won't forget: will-future: „... die du nicht vergessen wirst" / would not/wouldn't forget: conditional I: „... die du nicht vergessen würdest"*

Watching whales is very popular with (0) **tourists**. Vancouver Island in West Canada is a (1) **well**-known place for whale watching. Quite a few agencies offer such tours. And since the 1980s these tours (2) **have been** increasingly popular among tourists. You can choose between a tour on a motor or a sailing boat. Or you can even book a helicopter tour. Of course, this is really expensive but it (3) **offers** a completely different perspective. On the boat tours you get very (4) **close** to the giants of the ocean.

It is not dangerous because these animals are quite peaceful and never attack people. You could even paddle among them in a kayak. But this can be a bit risky because a whale's normal movements could (5) **easily** turn your kayak over. 'Swimming with the whales' would then be (6) **included** in the price! An experience you (7) **will not/won't/would not/wouldn't forget** for the rest of your life. Vancouver Island is indeed worth a visit.

Aufgabe 3

Hinweis: *Im vorgegebenen Text fehlt in regelmäßigen Abständen ein Wort. Lies den Text aber erst einmal ganz durch, um den Inhalt zu erfassen. Im zweiten Schritt konzentrierst du dich auf die Sätze mit den Lücken. Du kannst den Satz (in Gedanken) in deine Muttersprache übersetzen. Wenn dir klar ist, welches Wort inhaltlich in die Lücke passt, überlegst du, wie es auf Englisch heißt. Überprüfe im letzten Schritt, ob dieses Wort noch in eine bestimmte grammatikalische Form (z. B. Mehrzahl, Vergangenheit) gebracht werden muss.*

1. *Neben den Kilometern wird die Distanz auch noch in Meilen angegeben.*
4. *took place: Simple past, da Ereignis bereits vergangen („in 1984")*
6. *have to compete using similar dog sleds: müssen mit ähnlichen Hundeschlitten gegeneinander antreten*

The Yukon Quest is (0) **the** hardest dog-sled race in the world. To get from Whitehorse to Fairbanks, which is a distance of about 1,600 km or one thousand (1) **miles**, the fastest drivers need about eight days. Some sled drivers need a few days longer but every year (2) **there** are several who have to give up. Temperatures down to minus forty degrees and heavy winds (3) **make** this race a real challenge for the humans as well as for the dogs.

The first race (4) **took** place in February 1984. The name "Yukon Quest" goes back to the historical highway to the north. During the gold rush, about a hundred and fifty years (5) **ago**, the gold seekers used sleds like the ones the Inuit had. According to the race rules, participants in the Yukon Quest today (6) **have** to compete using similar dog sleds. The race is very popular, even in Europe. In 2002, it was won by a European for the first time.

C Reading Comprehension

Allgemeiner Hinweis: *In diesem Prüfungsteil stellst du dein Leseverstehen unter Beweis, indem du Aufgaben zum allgemeinen und detaillierten Verständnis bearbeitest. Beim ersten Durchlesen gewinnst du einen Überblick, worum es im Text geht. Konzentriere dich beim zweiten Lesen darauf, den Inhalt möglichst genau zu verstehen. Dann beginnst du mit dem dazugehörigen Aufgabenteil. Suche diejenigen Abschnitte oder Stellen im Text heraus, auf die sich die Aufgabe bezieht. Oft kannst du Satzteile, Angaben oder Wörter direkt aus dem Text als Antwort übernehmen, und auf diese Weise z. B. Rechtschreibfehler vermeiden.*

Vokabelhinweise:

Du findest nachfolgend eine Liste mit schwierigen Vokabeln aus dem Text. Zur Vorbereitung auf die Prüfung solltest du aber versuchen, möglichst viele Wörter aus dem Zusammenhang zu erschließen, sowie den Umgang mit dem Wörterbuch einzuüben. Aus Zeitgründen kannst du in der schriftlichen Prüfung nur die Wörter nachschlagen, die du unbedingt zum Verständnis benötigst.

Z. 3: Inuit: Selbstbezeichnung der Ureinwohner der kanadischen Arktis
Z. 6: remote: entlegen
Z. 10: to suffer from: an etwas leiden
Z. 10: principal: Schulleiter/in
Z. 11: conditions: Verhältnisse
Z. 12: majority: Mehrheit
Z. 15: temporary foster mother: Pflegemutter auf Zeit
Z. 16: promising results: erfolgsversprechende Ergebnisse
Z. 17: to benefit from sth: von etw profitieren
Z. 18: regular hours: reguläre Arbeitszeiten
Z. 20 f.: relationship: Beziehung
Z. 21: to continue: andauern, weiterbestehen
Z. 22: to deal with sth: mit etwas umgehen, sich um etwas kümmern
Z. 27: to assemble: zusammenbauen, montieren
Z. 28: to relieve: lindern
Z. 29: benefit: Vorteil
Z. 29: praise: Lob
Z. 30: self-confidence: Selbstvertrauen
Z. 36: digital access: Zugang zu digitalen Medien
Z. 37: to struggle: kämpfen
Z. 38: behavior: Verhalten
Z. 41: to transform sth: etwas umwandeln, verwandeln
Z. 42 f.: to receive: erhalten
Z. 43: award: Preis, Auszeichnung
Z. 43 f.: nomination: Vorschlag, Nominierung

Aufgabe 1

Hinweis: *In der folgenden Aufgabe sind dir unvollständige Sätze vorgegeben, die sich zwar auf den Lesetext beziehen, dort aber etwas anders formuliert sind. Lies dir zunächst die unvollständigen Sätze durch und frage dich: Wovon handelt der Satz? Welche Schlüsselwörter enthält er, die ich im Lesetext finden muss?*
Beispiel (0): Schlüsselwörter: Salluit, Quebec
Suche diese Wörter nun im Lesetext: Beispiel (0): "... Salluit, an Inuit village in northern Quebec. Salluit is a small village in the Canadian Arctic ..." (Z. 3 f.)
Schaue dir nun die Auswahlmöglichkeiten der Aufgabe an. Welches Wort oder welcher Satzteil deckt sich mit der Aussage im Lesetext bzw. welche Möglichkeit kann gar nicht stimmen? Im Beispiel ist die richtige Lösung „small village". Wenn du dir nicht

sicher bist, kann es helfen, Wörter im Wörterbuch nachzuschlagen, da man manchmal die Bedeutung verwechselt. Notfalls kannst du bei diesem Aufgabentyp auch in irgendeinem der Kästchen dein Häkchen setzen, vielleicht tippst du ja richtig.

1. In Salluit the climate is rough, sometimes the temperature … –25 °C.
   - ☐ is colder than
   - ☐ goes below
   - ☑ even reaches
   - ☐ is less than

   Hinweis: *Z. 6; „even reaches" = „erreicht sogar"*

2. The prize was handed over to Maggie MacDonnell in …
   - ☐ Quebec
   - ☐ Hawaii
   - ☑ Dubai
   - ☐ Salluit

   Hinweis: *Z. 42 f.*

3. The Global Teacher Prize has existed for … years.
   - ☐ two
   - ☑ four
   - ☐ seven
   - ☐ ten

   Hinweis: *Z. 44 f.*

4. The prize wants to show that teachers are … for society.
   - ☑ valuable
   - ☐ expensive
   - ☐ dangerous
   - ☐ responsible

   Hinweis: *Z. 45 f.; „valuable" = „wertvoll" = „important role"*

Aufgabe 2

Hinweis: *Im Lesetext ist jeder Absatz mit einem Buchstaben (A–F) gekennzeichnet. Deine Aufgabe ist es, die Fragen (1–5) genau dem Absatz zuzuordnen, der diese Frage beantwortet.*

1. *Z. 29 f.*
2. *Z. 15 f.*
3. *Z. 43 f.*
4. *Z. 7 f.*
5. *Z. 46 f.*

In which paragraph do you get the information that …

0. … Maggie MacDonnell did not have a director at her workplace in Salluit?	**B**
1. … the students feel better because of the positive feedback they get?	**D**
2. … some of Maggie's students live with her for a while?	**C**
3. … many teachers from all over the world wanted to become the world's best teacher?	**F**
4. … the furniture at her school was in need of repair?	**B**
5. … a politician from her home country honored Maggie's success?	**F**

Aufgabe 3

Hinweis: *Beantworte die Fragen zum Lesetext. Verwende das Wörterbuch, wenn du eine Frage nicht genau verstanden hast. Suche anschließend im Lesetext, wo du Informationen zu der Frage bekommst. Wenn du die Stelle gefunden hast, unterstreiche Schlüsselwörter oder Satzteile. Schreibe deine Lösung entweder in Stichpunkten oder als ganzen Satz auf.*

1. (only) by plane
   Hinweis: *Z. 4 f.*
2. books
   Hinweis: *Z. 8 f.*
3. on the sofa (in the living room) / in the living room
   Hinweis: *Z. 12 f.*

4. (a) community kitchen
   Hinweis: *Z. 23; „apart from“ = „außer“*
5. all the village's residents
   Hinweis: *Z. 28; „be allowed to“ = „dürfen“*
6. (the) half marathon (in Hawaii)
   Hinweis: *Z. 31 f.*

Aufgabe 4

Hinweis: *Bei dieser Aufgabe sind – ähnlich wie im Wörterbuch – verschiedene Wortbedeutungen vorgegeben. Die deutsche Bedeutung hängt davon ab, welche Funktion das englische Wort im Satz hat (z. B. Nomen – Namenwort, Verb – Tunwort, Adjektiv – Wiewort) und in welchem Sinnzusammenhang es im Text verwendet wird. Mithilfe der Zeilenangabe findest du das gesuchte Wort im Text. Lies und übersetze nun diesen Satz(teil), indem du jeweils eine der angegebenen Möglichkeiten verwendest. So kannst du die richtige Bedeutung herausfinden.*

1. face (line 7)
   - [ ] Fassade *(Nomen)*
   - [x] gegenüberstehen *(Verb)*
   - [ ] Gesicht *(Nomen)*
   - [ ] zeigen nach *(Verb)*

   Hinweis: *"this remote settlement faces some serious social problems" = „diese entlegene Siedlung steht einigen ernsthaften sozialen Problemen gegenüber“*

2. end (line 20)
   - [x] aufhören *(Verb)*
   - [ ] beenden *(Verb)*
   - [ ] Ende *(Nomen)*
   - [ ] Ziel *(Nomen)*

   Hinweis: *"as a teacher in a small Arctic village your day never ends" = „für einen Lehrer in einem kleinen arktischen Dorf hört der Tag nie auf/endet der Tag nie“*

3. service (line 25)
   - ☐ Bedienung *(Nomen)*
   - ☑ Dienstleistung *(Nomen)*
   - ☐ instand halten *(Verb)*
   - ☐ Wartung *(Nomen)*

   Hinweis: *"and also provides a useful service to the community" = „und stellt der Gemeinde auch eine nützliche Dienstleistung zur Verfügung"*

4. spend (line 31)
   - ☐ Ausgabe *(Nomen)*
   - ☐ ausgeben *(Verb)*
   - ☐ verbrauchen *(Verb)*
   - ☑ verbringen *(Verb)*

   Hinweis: *"Ms. MacDonnell spends a lot of time as a coach for the Salluit Running Club" = „Ms. MacDonnell verbringt viel Zeit als Trainerin des Laufvereins von Salluit"*

5. level (line 34)
   - ☐ eben *(Adjektiv)*
   - ☑ Ebene *(Nomen)*
   - ☐ gleichmachen *(Verb)*
   - ☐ Pegel *(Nomen)*

   Hinweis: *"connect on a person-to-person level" = „sich auf einer persönlichen Ebene verbinden"*

D Text Production

Allgemeiner Hinweis: *Lies dir beide Aufgabenstellungen erst einmal gut durch. Entscheide dich dann entweder für den Brief oder für die Bildergeschichte. Berücksichtige die Vorgaben, die in der Aufgabenstellung enthalten sind. Achte auf einen klaren Satzbau, abwechslungsreichen Wortschatz sowie die Rechtschreibung. Verwende das Wörterbuch, und kontrolliere immer wieder, ob dein Text sprachlich und inhaltlich schlüssig und verständlich ist. Du erhältst sowohl für den Inhalt als auch auf die sprachliche Gestaltung Punkte. Halte dich an den vorgeschriebenen Umfang, schreibe leserlich und achte auf eine saubere äußere Form. Die folgenden Texte sind Lösungsbeispiele.*

Hinweis: *Bei dieser Schreibaufgabe liegt ein Brief von Sam vor, dem du ebenfalls in Form eines Briefes antworten sollst. In deinem Antwortbrief gehst du auf die Dinge ein, die dein Brieffreund von dir wissen will. Überlege dir ebenfalls, was du über Sam erfahren willst.*
Im ersten Schritt gehst du Sams Brief in Ruhe durch und markierst, was er von dir wissen will. Sammle Ideen, was du darauf antworten könntest. Mache dir dann Gedanken, welche Fragen du an Sam hast.
Beginne nun mit dem Schreiben, indem du das Datum notierst und die Anrede verfasst. Was den Aufbau betrifft, kannst du dich an Sams Brief orientieren.
Wähle für den Hauptteil aus deiner „Ideensammlung" die Punkte aus, zu denen dir inhaltlich und sprachlich viel einfällt. Schreibe in ganzen, vollständigen Sätzen. Kontrolliere deinen Brief am Ende noch einmal: Ist er interessant zu lesen, vollständig und verständlich? Hast du dich verabschiedet?

30 June 2018

Hi Sam,

Thanks for your letter! My name is Tobias, I'm 16 years old and I live in Regensburg. This is a very old city in the east of Bavaria. The Danube flows through it, which is the second longest river in Europe.
I have a lot of hobbies. Now in summer I like to be outside with my friends and do various kinds of activities. What I like best is going to the high ropes course. We have such courses in Regensburg but also in other places in Bavaria. Have you ever tried it? You climb up trees and move from one tree to the next on planks, pendant bridges or ropes. It is very exciting but also safe because your body is always fixed with a rope. I also like swimming and cycling along the Danube.
You also asked about my plans for the future. I'll graduate from school soon, but I haven't found an apprenticeship place yet. I want to become a carpenter.
I'd like to have a penfriend in Canada because I'm interested in this beautiful country, and I'd like to improve my English by writing to you.
What is it like to live in Kelowna? Is it close to the sea? Do you also learn a foreign language at school?
I'm looking forward to your reply!

Take care,

Tobias *(224 words)*

Hinweis: *Bei dieser Schreibaufgabe sollst du die Informationen und Ideen, die du den sechs Bildern entnehmen kannst, in Form einer zusammenhängenden Geschichte erzählen. Betrachte zunächst jedes einzelne Bild genau und notiere dir einige Schlüsselwörter dazu. Auch Einzelheiten können für die Handlung wichtig sein. Überlege dann, welche Bilder du der Einleitung, dem Hauptteil und dem Schluss zuordnen würdest. Ändere dabei aber keinesfalls die vorgegebene Reihenfolge der Bilder!*
Der Hauptteil beginnt normalerweise bei dem Bild, ab dem die Geschichte spannend wird, weil etwas Unerwartetes passiert. Diesen Teil solltest du ausführlich erzählen. Überlege dir schließlich, wie deine Geschichte endet.
Achte darauf, die Überschrift und den Anfangssatz aus der Aufgabe zu übernehmen. Lass die Personen in der Geschichte miteinander sprechen („wörtliche Rede") um deine Erzählung lebendig zu machen. Die folgende Geschichte ist eine Beispiellösung. So könnte z. B. die Keksdose auch eine Packung Chips sein.

A hungry squirrel

One day in winter Katie and her brother Jim were sitting in the igloo which they had built next to their house. Inside the igloo it was not very cold, so they sat on their jackets while eating cookies out of a tin. When their mom called them inside for dinner, they forgot to take the tin and their jackets with them.
Early the next morning they had to get ready for school. Their mom pointed at the empty coat-hooks and asked "Where are your jackets, kids?" "I think we have left them in the igloo", Katie remembered and went out into the garden with Jim and mom. The jackets were still inside the igloo. But what was that? A little squirrel was sitting on one of the jackets, eating cookies from the tin and leaving crumbs all over. The jackets had become quite messy. At first Katie was upset and wanted to chase away the squirrel, but then she felt sorry for the hungry animal and so the family allowed it to finish its meal.
However, Katie and Jim had no idea how to get to school without their warm jackets!

(195 words)

Notenschlüssel

Notenstufen	1	2	3	4	5	6
Punkte	80–68	67–55	54–41	40–27	26–13	12–0

Qualifizierender Abschluss der Mittelschule Bayern 2019
Lösungen – Englisch

A Listening Comprehension

Allgemeiner Hinweis: *Jeder Hörtext wird zweimal vorgespielt. Du hast in den Pausen vor und nach den Texten ausreichend Zeit, um die Aufgabenstellungen durchzulesen bzw. die Lösungen einzutragen.*

Aufgabe 1

Receptionist: Portobello Hotel. Can I help you?

Marcus: Hello. Yes, I'd like to know if you have any rooms available at the end of August.

Receptionist: Let me have a look. End of August. OK, when were you thinking of coming exactly?

Marcus: Um … August 28.

Receptionist: OK. And for how many nights?

Marcus: Two.

Receptionist: Right. Is that a single or a double?

Marcus: Double, please.

Receptionist: Yes, that looks fine.

Marcus: Great. I see on the internet you charge £ 110 a night for a double. Is that right?

Receptionist: In winter, yes. But in summer they're £ 130, I'm afraid.

Marcus: Mmm. OK. And does that include breakfast?

Receptionist: Yes, of course.

Marcus: It says here that you're very close to the Underground.

Receptionist: Yes, five minutes on foot from the tube station Holland Park.

Marcus: Is that the Central Line?

Receptionist: Yes, so it's six stops to Oxford Circus.

Marcus: OK. Great.

Receptionist: So, shall we book that for you?

Marcus: Yes, please.

Receptionist: Leaving on August 30?

Marcus: That's right.

Receptionist: OK. Could I take your name, please?

Hinweis: *Hier findest du unvollständige Aussagen, die du durch die Informationen aus dem Hörtext ergänzen sollst. Lies die Sätze zunächst genau durch und markiere*

Schlüsselwörter in den Aussagen (z. B. 1. come/August, 3. double room/in summer). Achte während des Hörens auf diese Schlüsselwörter und ergänze die Lücken im Satz mit der jeweils passenden Information aus dem Hörtext.

Vokabelhinweis:
on foot (Z. 18) = zu Fuß

1. Laura and Marcus want to come to London on August **(the) 28(th)**.
   Hinweis: *Z. 6*
2. They want to stay at the Portobello Hotel for two **nights**.
   Hinweis: *Z. 8*
3. A double room costs £ **130** in summer.
   Hinweis: *Z. 14*
4. The hotel is five minutes **on foot** from the tube station Holland Park.
   Hinweis: *Z. 18*
5. From Holland Park it's six **stops** to Oxford Circus.
   Hinweis: *Z. 18ff.*
6. Laura and Marcus are leaving on August **(the) 30(th)**.
   Hinweis: *Z. 24f.*

Aufgabe 2

Woman: Hello there. How can I help?
Laura: Er … yeah … we've heard about something called a London Pass. Could you tell us what it is exactly?
Woman: Well, it's like a smart card. It gets you into tourist attractions in London without having to pay in cash every time.
Laura: OK. So places like the Tower of London?
Woman: Yes, exactly. And the other thing is that you don't have to queue to get in. You just walk to the front and go through.
Laura: Oh, that's good. How much does it cost?
Woman: £43 a day.
Marcus: Is a day 24 hours from when I buy the pass or is it … is it …?
Woman: No, it's a calendar day. So if you don't pick up your card until late in the afternoon you've lost quite a lot of money.
Laura: Mmm. OK. And can we get one here, right now?
Woman: Yes, you can. But it's 1 o'clock so …
Marcus: … and when do you open in the morning?
Woman: 10 am.

Marcus: So we could order it now and pick it up tomorrow at 10?
Woman: Yes, of course.
Laura (to Marcus): Let's do that, shall we?
Woman: So that's two, is it?
Marcus: Yes, please.

Hinweis: *In der Aufgabe sind Sätze vorgegeben, die sich vom jeweiligen Satz im Hörtext durch genau ein Wort unterscheiden. Konzentriere dich auf diese Sätze mit dem Ziel, während des Zuhörens die entsprechende Textstelle zu erkennen. Streiche das Wort, das sich vom Hörtext unterscheidet, sobald du es erkennst.*

Vokabelhinweis:
to queue (Z. 7) = sich in der Warteschlange anstellen

1. It gets you into ~~terrific~~ attractions in London.
   Hinweis: *Z. 4*
2. And the ~~best~~ thing is that you don't have to queue to get in.
   Hinweis: *Z. 7*
3. So if you don't pick up your card until late in the ~~evening~~ …
   Hinweis: *Z. 12 f.*
4. And can ~~you~~ get one here?
   Hinweis: *Z. 14*
5. So we could order it now and pick it up tomorrow at ~~11~~?
   Hinweis: *Z. 18*

Aufgabe 3

Receptionist: Hello.
Marcus: Hello. Could you help me with some directions, please?
Receptionist: Yes, sure. Where do you want to go?
Marcus: The Tower of London.
Receptionist: On the tube?
Marcus: Yeah. And it says here that the nearest station is Tower Hill.
Receptionist: OK.
Marcus: So shall we go this way round … on the Circle Line or …?
Receptionist: You can do. But it takes quite a long time. And you have to change once.
Marcus: OK. What would you suggest?

Receptionist: Well, if you take the Central Line and go to Bank, that's the station here, it's much quicker and you don't have to change.

Marcus: Oh, I see. That's ... one, two, three ... eleven stations.

Receptionist: Yeah. The only problem is ...

Marcus: Yeah?

Receptionist: You have to walk a bit from Bank station to the Tower.

Marcus: OK. How far?

Receptionist: Um ... about fifteen minutes I'd say. But all in all it's probably quicker than the other route, you know, going round here on the Circle Line.

Marcus: And we get some exercise, too.

Receptionist: Yeah, that as well!

Hinweis: *Um die Fragen beantworten zu können, musst du sie inhaltlich verstehen („which?" = „welche?", „how long?" = „wie lange?"). Nur so weißt du, auf welche Informationen du während des Hörens achten musst. Ein weiterer Anhaltspunkt sind Schlüsselwörter aus den Fragen („line" = „U-Bahn-Linie"; walk, Bank station, Tower), da diese auch im Hörtext vorkommen und deine Aufmerksamkeit auf die jeweils richtige Textstelle lenken.*

Vokabelhinweise:

directions (Z. 2) = Wegbeschreibung
on the tube (Z. 5) = mit der U-Bahn
to change (Z. 9) = umsteigen
to suggest (Z. 11) = vorschlagen

1. Central Line
   Hinweis: *Z. 11 f.*
2. 15 minutes
   Hinweis: *Z. 17 ff.*

Aufgabe 4

Guest: Your last day, then?

Marcus: Yes, it is. Have you just arrived?

Guest: Yes, last night.

Laura: And how long are you staying?

Guest: For a week. We come every year actually. And always in August.

Marcus: You must know London very well.

Guest: Yes, we do. We love it here.

Laura: And do you go sightseeing when you're here?

Guest: Well, we know all the main attractions very well; the London Eye, the Crown Jewels and so on.

Laura: Yeah.

Guest: Now we like going to museums. There're so many of them in London. And most of them are free.

Marcus: You mean the British Museum?

Guest: Well, that's the most famous one. But there are others. The Science Museum is great. And the Natural History Museum, too.

Laura: So what have you got planned for today?

Guest: Well, this morning we want to go to the Museum of London.

Marcus: The Museum of London? Where's that?

Guest: Not far from St Paul's Cathedral. So, easy to get to from here.

Marcus: Well, have a good day.

Guest: Thanks. You have a good flight, too.

Marcus & Laura: Thanks.

Hinweis: *Entscheide bei dieser Aufgabe, welche Aussagen zum Hörtext richtig oder falsch sind. Beachte, dass die Aussagen in der Aufgabe nur sinngemäß formuliert sind, d. h. mit anderen Worten als im Hörtext (z. B. sights ↔ attractions, travel home by plane ↔ flight).*

Vokabelhinweis:
museums … are free (Z. 12 f.) = hier: freier Eintritt

	T	F
1. The guest arrived at the hotel this morning. **Hinweis:** *Z. 2 f.*	☐	☑
2. The guest wants to stay in London for a week. **Hinweis:** *Z. 4 f.*	☑	☐

	T	F
3. The guest knows the main sights in London well. **Hinweis:** *Z. 9*	✓	☐
4. All museums in London are free. **Hinweis:** *Z. 12 f.*	☐	✓
5. The British Museum is the most famous museum in London. **Hinweis:** *Z. 14 f.*	✓	☐
6. This morning the guest wants to go to St Paul's Cathedral. **Hinweis:** *Z. 18*	☐	✓
7. Laura and Marcus travel home by plane. **Hinweis:** *Z. 22*	✓	☐

B Use of English

Allgemeiner Hinweis: *Anders als in den Vorjahren ist der Prüfungsteil diesmal so gegliedert, dass pro Aufgabe immer nur ein Teilgebiet geprüft wird: Wortschatz (Aufgaben 1, 2), ein Grammatikbereich (Aufgaben 3, 4) sowie ein Dialog (Aufgabe 5). Beachte, dass du kein Wörterbuch verwenden darfst.*

Aufgabe 1

Hinweis: *In dieser Aufgabe geht es um Präpositionen und Konjunktionen. Welches Wort du verwenden musst, ergibt sich aus dem Satzzusammenhang. Die Präpositionen sind oft Teil einer festen Verbindung.*

1. *born on … = geboren am … (Präposition)*
2. *good at … = gut in …(Präposition)*
3. *when = als / although = obwohl (Konjunktionen)*
4. *get a job as a … = eine Arbeit als … bekommen (Präposition)*

The US rock singer Gwen Stefani was born (0) **in** Orange County, California (1) **on** October 3rd, 1969. She has got three brothers and sisters and they are all good (2) **at** music. Eric, one of Gwen's brothers, started the band called *No Doubt*. Gwen became the band's lead singer (3) **when/although** she was only 18. In 1995 Eric left the band because he got a job (4) **as** a cartoon artist.

Aufgabe 2

Hinweis: *Bei dieser Wortschatzaufgabe wird das gesuchte Wort mit einer Definition umschrieben. Der Anfangsbuchstabe und die Anzahl der Buchstaben sind als Hilfe vorgegeben. Notiere die einzelnen Buchstaben des gesuchten Wortes auf den vorgegebenen Strichen.*
2. return ticket = Hin- und Rückfahrkarte

1. s**tation**
2. r**eturn** ticket
3. l**ate**
4. p**assenger**

Aufgabe 3

Hinweis: *Hier sind überwiegend zusammengesetzte Wörter mit „some" und „any" vorgegeben. Der Unterschied liegt in der grammatikalischen Verwendung. Vereinfacht gilt folgende Regel: „Some" verwendest du in Aussagen und bejahten Sätzen, „any" in Fragen und verneinten Sätzen.*
0. everyone = jede(r), hier auch: alle
1. anywhere = nirgendwo (wegen Verneinung „could<u>n't</u> see Tim anywhere")
2. everywhere = überall
3. something = etwas
4. anything = nichts (wegen Verneinung „had<u>n't</u> had anything")

Susan and Tim went surfing with some friends and (0) **everyone** had a lot of fun. Suddenly Susan couldn't see Tim (1) **anywhere**. She looked for him (2) **everywhere**. Then she saw him at a hamburger stall. He was buying (3) **something** to eat because he hadn't had (4) **anything** for breakfast.

Aufgabe 4

Hinweis: *Dies ist eine Aufgabe zum Grammatikbereich „tenses" – Zeiten. In Klammern ist die Grundform eines englischen Verbs (Tunworts) vorgegeben. Lies dir zunächst die zusammengehörenden Sätze jedes Absatzes genau durch, da zeitlich zum Teil Bezug auf den vorherigen bzw. nachfolgenden Satz genommen wird. Unterstreiche außerdem Signalwörter, die darauf hinweisen, welche englische Zeitform verwendet werden muss. Beachte auch Besonderheiten, z. B. im „simple present" (he, she, it → Verb +„s").*
1. every year (Signalwort), the club offer<u>s</u> („simple present")

2. *ever (Signalwort für „present perfect")*
3. *last year (Signalwort für „simple past")*
4. *this time (hier: Signalwort für „simple present")*

Brenda (0) **is** a member of a youth club. Every year the club (1) **offers** summer activities.
At the moment Brenda and her friends are sitting on the train to Brighton. A friendly lady starts talking to them. She asks Brenda, "(2) **Have** you ever **been** to Brighton?"
Brenda answers, "Unfortunately not. It's my first time. Last year I was on holiday near Brighton but I (3) **did not/didn't go** to Brighton itself. So this time I (4) **want** to do some sightseeing."

Aufgabe 5

Hinweis: *In dem Dialog sind die Fragen, die Chris stellt, bereits in der richtigen Reihenfolge angegeben. Du musst nur noch die passenden Antworten (A–H) auf Alex' Seite finden und in die Tabelle eintragen. Achte darauf, dass der Dialog logisch ist und einen Sinn ergibt.*

Vokabelhinweis:
to spend money = Geld ausgeben

0	1	2	3	4	**5**
C	D	B	F	E	**H**

C Reading Comprehension

Allgemeiner Hinweis: *In diesem Prüfungsteil stellst du dein Leseverstehen unter Beweis, indem du Aufgaben zum allgemeinen und detaillierten Verständnis bearbeitest. Beim ersten Durchlesen gewinnst du einen Überblick, worum es im Text geht. Konzentriere dich beim zweiten Lesen darauf, den Inhalt möglichst genau zu verstehen. Dann beginnst du mit dem dazugehörigen Aufgabenteil. Suche diejenigen Abschnitte oder Stellen im Text heraus, auf die sich die jeweilige Aufgabe bezieht. Vieles kannst du direkt aus dem Text als Antwort übernehmen, und auf diese Weise z. B. Rechtschreibfehler vermeiden.*

Vokabelhinweise:
Du findest nachfolgend eine Liste mit schwierigen Vokabeln aus dem Text. Zur Vorbereitung auf die Prüfung solltest du aber versuchen, möglichst viele Wörter aus dem Zusammenhang zu erschließen, sowie den Umgang mit dem Wörterbuch einzuüben. Aus Zeitgründen kannst du in der schriftlichen Prüfung nur die Wörter nachschlagen, die du unbedingt zum Verständnis benötigst.

Z. 1: capsule = Kapsel, hier: Gondel
Z. 9: breathtaking = atemberaubend
Z. 11: to be scared = Angst haben
Z. 18: to board = einsteigen
Z. 20: observation wheel = Riesenrad
Z. 29: to take a flight: hier = eine Fahrt machen
Z. 30: occasion = Anlass
Z. 30: to hire = mieten
Z. 33: location = Lage
Z. 33 f.: to use for demonstrations = hier: auf sich oder ein Anliegen aufmerksam machen
Z. 38: vision = Sicht, hier: Vision (= Vorstellung)
Z. 39: aim = Ziel

Aufgabe 1

Hinweis: *Der Lesetext ist in Absätze unterteilt – die genaue Unterteilung kannst du den Zeilenangaben in der Tabelle entnehmen. Jedem Absatz soll nun eine Überschrift (A–G) zugeordnet werden. Lies dir jeweils einen Absatz des Lesetextes durch und vergleiche ihn mit der Auswahl an Überschriften. Falls du nicht sofort die passende Überschrift erkennst, kannst du zuerst die Überschriften der anderen Absätze zuordnen.*

Vokabelhinweise:
A: difficulties = Schwierigkeiten, to construct: bauen
E: attraction = Attraktion, Sehenswürdigkeit
F: offer = Angebot
G: exciting: aufregend, experience = Erfahrung

lines 1–15	lines 16–19	lines 20–25	lines 26–32	lines 33–36	lines 37–40
C	G	A	F	B	E

Aufgabe 2

Hinweis: *Entscheide auf Grundlage des Lesetextes, ob die Aussagen 1–4 richtig oder falsch sind oder es im Lesetext gar keinen Beleg für sie gibt. Nimm dir Zeit, die vorgegebenen Sätze zu verstehen, da sie grammatikalisch manchmal nicht ganz einfach sind.*

	T	F	N
1. The London Eye moves very fast. **Hinweis:** *Z. 4 f. („slow climb")*	☐	☑	☐
2. Building the London Eye was finished before the year 2000. **Hinweis:** *Das „London Eye" war 1999 fertig. (Z. 24 f.)*	☑	☐	☐
3. A man was arrested after his protest in 2004. **Hinweis:** *was arrested = wurde verhaftet*	☐	☐	☑
4. The London Eye is still the highest observation wheel in the world. **Hinweis:** *still = immer noch; es gibt inzwischen ein höheres Riesenrad (Z. 37 f.)*	☐	☑	☐

Aufgabe 3

Hinweis: *Beantworte die Fragen mithilfe des Textes in Stichpunkten. Durchsuche den Lesetext nach der jeweiligen Antwort. Es kann hilfreich sein, die entscheidende Textstelle farblich zu markieren.*

1. half an hour / 30 minutes
   Hinweis: *Z. 18*
2. seven / 7 years
   Hinweis: *Z. 21*
3. March 2000
   Hinweis: *Z. 26*
4. 15,000 / 15 000
   Hinweis: *Z. 29*
5. birthday(s) / Christmas / wedding(s)
   Hinweis: *Von den drei möglichen Beispielen müssen zwei genannt werden. Pro Beispiel gibt es 1 Punkt, also insgesamt 2 Punkte.*
   what kind of event = welche Art von Veranstaltung; Z. 29 ff.

Aufgabe 4

Hinweis: *Hier wird nach Informationen aus dem Text gefragt. Stelle sicher, dass du die Fragen vollständig verstehst, indem du z. B. unbekannten Wortschatz im Wörterbuch nachschlägst. Die Reihenfolge der Fragen folgt dem Textaufbau, d. h., die Antwort auf Frage 1 steht im oberen Teil des Lesetextes, usw. Sobald du den Satz im Text gefunden hast, der die Antwort auf die zugehörige Frage beinhaltet, solltest du diesen richtig und in voller Länge abschreiben.*

1. If the weather is clear, you'll be able to see Windsor Castle, 38 km away.
   Hinweis: *Z. 14 f.*
2. From here cars, buses and taxis look like children's toys.
   Hinweis: *Z. 16 f.; vehicles = Fahrzeuge*
3. Over 1,700 people from five countries worked on it.
   Hinweis: *Z. 21 f.; people = Menschen, Leute*
4. But three and a half million people came.
   Hinweis: *Z. 28: Es wird nach der tatsächlichen Anzahl von Besuchern („actually visited") gefragt und nicht nach der erhofften Besucherzahl. Im Text wird auch die Angabe „Jahr" (year) statt „12 Monate" (12 months) verwendet.*
5. And for around £ 2,000 you can celebrate your wedding in a private capsule decorated with flowers.
   Hinweis: *Z. 31 f.*

D Text Production

Allgemeiner Hinweis: *Lies dir beide Aufgabenstellungen erst einmal gut durch. Entscheide dich dann entweder für die E-Mail oder für die Bildergeschichte. Berücksichtige die Vorgaben, die in der Aufgabenstellung enthalten sind. Achte auf einen klaren Satzbau, abwechslungsreichen Wortschatz sowie die Rechtschreibung. Verwende das Wörterbuch, und kontrolliere immer wieder, ob dein Text sprachlich richtig und inhaltlich schlüssig und verständlich ist. Du erhältst sowohl für den Inhalt als auch auf die sprachliche Gestaltung Punkte. Halte dich an den vorgeschriebenen Umfang, schreibe leserlich und achte auf eine saubere äußere Form. Die folgenden Texte sind Lösungsbeispiele.*

Hinweis: *Halte dich den Inhalt betreffend an die verbindlichen Angaben der Aufgabe, die du durch eigene Ideen ergänzt. Eine genaue Anleitung, wie du beim Schreiben der E-Mail vorgehst, findest du im Kompetenzbereich „Schreiben" im Trainingsteil des Aufgabenbandes.*
Lies die Aufgabenstellung genau durch: Der Adressat ist ein Hotel in London, dem du wegen einer vergessenen Reisetasche schreibst. Du wählst also einen formellen, höflichen Stil. Verwende eine geeignete Anrede und Schlussformel und nach Möglichkeit Langformen (z. B. „I am").
In der Aufgabe sind die Inhalte, die du erwähnen musst, bereits auf Deutsch aufgelistet. Gehe sie der Reihe nach durch. Du musst sie jedoch noch teilweise ausschmücken, indem du z. B. eine Zimmernummer erfindest oder angibst, wo die Tasche vermutlich vergessen wurde. Schlage unbekannten Wortschatz im Wörterbuch nach.
Beginne nun mit dem Schreiben. Solange du über euren zurückliegenden Aufenthalt berichtest, solltest du die „simple past"-Vergangenheit verwenden. Bei der Beschreibung der Tasche und bei der Bitte um Nachsendung ist die „simple present"-Gegenwart angemessen.
Kontrolliere zum Schluss deinen Text. Beträgt der Umfang ca. 100 Wörter? Hast du alle Angaben berücksichtigt? Hast du leserlich und verständlich geschrieben? Hast du an Anrede und Verabschiedung gedacht?

Dear Madam or Sir,

My parents and I were guests in your hotel and we enjoyed our stay with you very much. I am writing because we left behind one of our bags at your hotel when we checked out yesterday. We believe that we left the bag in room number 304 on the third floor. It could be in the wardrobe. It is a dark blue sports bag with a large white tiger on one side. There are some hiking socks and a travel guide about Wales in it. Could you please look for our bag and send it to our address (see the bottom of this email)? We would pay for the shipping costs, of course.
Please reply soon. Thank you very much in advance.

Kind regards,

Tim Baumann
Hauptstr. 62
97070 Würzburg
Germany

(136 words)

Hinweis: *Als Schreibanlass werden dir eine Zeichnung („picture") und Angaben in Form von Stichpunkten („prompts") vorgelegt. Verwende diese für eine schlüssige Geschichte. Wie du dabei genau vorgehst, kannst du im Kompetenzbereich „Schreiben" im Trainingsteil des Aufgabenbandes nachlesen.*
Betrachte zuerst das Bild: Zwei Jungen entdecken in einem Geschäft einen gut gefüllten Geldbeutel, der offen auf dem Boden liegt. Überlege nun, wie Bild und Stichwörter zusammenhängen. Wie könnte es zu dieser Situation gekommen sein und wie könnte die Geschichte weitergehen? Notiere nun deine Ideen und wähle die besten aus.
Wichtig ist die Angabe „gemeinsame Entscheidung", da sie den Höhepunkt der Geschichte darstellt. Sie sollte sich aus den Gedanken und Gesprächen der beiden Jungen ergeben: Entweder sind sich die beiden von Anfang an einig, wie sie mit dem Fund umgehen wollen (behalten oder zurückgeben), oder eben nicht. Auch der Stichpunkt „Vorgang an der Kasse" lässt verschiedene Möglichkeiten offen. Der Kunde an der Kasse könnte seinen Geldbeutel suchen. Die Teenager beschließen, ihren Einkauf mit dem Geld aus dem Fund zu bezahlen oder sie sind ehrliche Finder und geben den Geldbeutel an der Kasse ab.
Schreibe nun die Geschichte im vorgeschriebenen Umfang und gliedere sie in Einleitung, Hauptteil und Schluss. Überschrift und Einleitung sind bereits vorgegeben. Daraus sind sowohl die Namen der Hauptfiguren (Paul und Jake) als auch die zu verwendende Zeitform („simple past") ersichtlich. Nutze bei Bedarf ein Wörterbuch. Verwende bei Gedanken und Gesprächen die wörtliche Rede (z. B. Paul said: "…").
Überprüfe zum Schluss, ob deine Geschichte den geforderten Umfang (ca. 100 Wörter) hat und aus Einleitung, Hauptteil (mit Spannungsbogen) und Schluss besteht. Sind alle notwendigen Informationen enthalten? Enthält sie wörtliche Rede? Ist deine Geschichte gut lesbar und nachvollziehbar, auch wenn man das Bild und die Angaben nicht kennt?
Der folgende Text ist eine Beispiellösung. Er ist bewusst umfangreicher gehalten, als in der Aufgabe gefordert. Dies soll dir Ideen für deine eigene Geschichte geben und es dir ermöglichen, deinen Wortschatz zu erweitern.

Lost and found

Last Saturday afternoon Paul and Jake were in a games shop. Suddenly Jake saw a wallet.
"Look at this, Paul, there's a wallet on the floor!" Jake exclaimed and thought he should pick it up before anybody else did.
"Hush, be quiet" Paul said.
Jake picked up the wallet. There were some credit cards and some 50 pound notes in it.

Paul said: "You're not thinking of keeping it?"
"Why not?" Jake answered.
"Someone is missing it!" Paul said.
"Ah, come on! I just found this great new video game and I don't have the money to buy it. With the cash in that wallet I could ..."
Paul said: "Forget about it! We have to report that we found it."
"OK, OK, you're right." Jake gave in.
At the check-out a customer was very upset. He wanted to pay but couldn't find his wallet. He was so happy when the boys arrived at the check-out with it. As a reward the man asked them to choose one of the video games. Jake knew exactly which one to take! *(165 words)*

Notenschlüssel

Notenstufen	1	2	3	4	5	6
Punkte	80–68	67–55	54–41	40–27	26–13	12–0

Qualifizierender Abschluss der Mittelschule Bayern 2020
Lösungen – Englisch

A Listening Comprehension

Allgemeiner Hinweis: *Die Hörtexte werden in der Prüfung jeweils zweimal vorgespielt. In den Pausen vor und nach den Texten hast du ausreichend Zeit, um die Aufgaben durchzulesen bzw. die Lösungen einzutragen.*

Aufgabe 1

Flight attendant: Ladies and gentlemen, we'll soon be landing in Melbourne. Please put your seats in an upright position and fasten your seatbelts.

Steve: Aaah … at last!

Anna: Yes, it has been a long flight, hasn't it? Do you live in Melbourne?

Steve: I do, but I spent the last six months working in Europe. What about you?

Ben: We're on holiday. We want to learn how to dive so we've booked a 5-day beginners' course in Townsville. It starts next Thursday. It costs nine-hundred and thirty dollars each! But it's always been our dream to go diving in Australia.

Steve: So you're not staying in Melbourne then?

Anna: Oh yes, we are. We've booked a hotel for three nights.

Steve: Have you heard of the Skydeck? That's a great starting place for visitors.

Ben: What's that?

Steve: It's a viewing platform in the city centre. It's on the 88th floor of a skyscraper. On a good day you can see the whole city!

Anna: Wow, sounds great.

Steve: It is. It's open almost all day, but if you go there late afternoon you can watch the sunset and see the city lights after dark. It's very impressive. But you shouldn't be afraid of heights because you're standing on a glass floor looking down nearly 300 metres. It's south of the river, near Princes Bridge.

Anna: Hmm … someone told us about Phillip Island …

Steve: Ah, the penguin island.

Ben: Is it worth a visit?

Steve: Yeah, sure. It's about 80 kilometres south of Melbourne.

Anna: Oh, so far away.

Steve: It's not that bad. It's a nice trip by ferry from Melbourne. One leaves every hour and you don't need to book.

Anna: That sounds good. Let's do that tomorrow. And then on the next day we can go shopping …

Hinweis: *Ergänze die Lücken mit den passenden Wörtern aus dem Hörtext. Oft helfen dir auch Schlüsselwörter in den Lückensätzen (z. B. „learn how to"; „starts on", „platform"), das fehlende Wort im Hörtext zu erkennen.*

1. dive
   Hinweis: *Z. 6*
2. Thursday
   Hinweis: *Z. 7*
3. viewing
   Hinweis: *Z. 13*
4. late afternoon / sunset / after dark
   Hinweis: *Z. 16f.*
5. glass floor
   Hinweis: *Z. 18*
6. south
   Hinweis: *Z. 23*
7. ferry
   Hinweis: *Z. 25*

Aufgabe 2

Guide: Ladies and gentlemen, Welcome to Phillip Island.
Here you can experience one of Australia's most famous attractions, our penguins. About 32,000 of the world's smallest penguins live on Phillip Island. They spend 80 per cent of their time in the ocean hunting fish, but each night at sunset they come back to the island. Then they walk one and a half kilometers back to their colony. This is the famous Penguin Parade. It's sure to be the highlight of your visit.
Please don't leave the viewing areas and the paths during the parade. If you get too close to the penguins, they will get scared and will not come back here. Photography and filming are not allowed either because the penguins have sensitive eyes and the bright flashes from your cameras can damage them. But you can download our free Phillip Island app: there you will find detailed information, photos and short films which you can keep or even share with your friends.
I would also like to mention the Penguin Foundation which collects money and protects the penguin colony on Phillip Island. It also gives medical care for sick and injured penguins in our small penguin hospital. To do that the Foundation needs about $ 45,000 a year. You can join today for as little as $ 15 a year and

adopt a penguin. Every cent goes directly to penguin projects to care for the little animals. The gates to the viewing areas will only open an hour before the arrival of the penguins, so there will be enough time to go to the visitor centre, one of the cafés or the souvenir shop. That's it for now, we hope you enjoy your stay on Phillip Island. Maybe we can welcome you again on your next visit to Phillip Island …

Hinweis: *Bei dieser Aufgabe reicht es aus, wenn du für deine Antworten Stichpunkte aus dem Hörtext verwendest. Die Fragen werden im Text nacheinander beantwortet. Da in den Fragen und im Hörtext dieselben Schlüsselwörter (z. B. „spend"/ „per cent of their time") vorkommen, erkennst du rasch, wann du besonders gut zuhören musst.*

1. 80

   Hinweis: *Z. 4*
2. (They will) get scared / (They) will not/won't come back

   Hinweis: *Z. 9*
3. (bright) flashes (from cameras) / photography / filming

   Hinweis: *Z. 9 ff.*
4. collect money / protect the (penguin) colony/ (give) medical care (for sick and injured penguins)

   Hinweis: *Z. 14 ff.*
5. 15

   Hinweis: *Z. 17 f.*
6. an/one/1 hour

   Hinweis: *Z. 20 f.*

Aufgabe 3

Receptionist: Good morning, what can I do for you?

Ben: It's our last full day in Melbourne. Do you have any tips what we could do?

Receptionist: Hmm, why don't you visit Melbourne Cricket Ground? It's Australia's biggest stadium with more than 100,000 seats.

Ben: Cricket? I don't know ... It's not my favourite sport.

Receptionist: It's not just a cricket stadium. You can watch other sports there, too, for example rugby or Australian football. In fact, there's an Australian football match today.

Anna: Australian football?

Receptionist: It's a great sport – a mix of football and rugby. It's very popular in Australia. Today my favourite team, the Richmond Tigers, are playing against the Brisbane Bears. Oh wait, that's next week. Today, they're playing against Sydney. The match begins at 5.45 in the afternoon.

Ben: That sounds great. Then we've got time to do something else before.

Receptionist: You can also do a guided tour of the stadium, which includes a visit to the players' changing rooms and a walk on the field. You'll have to do it in the morning, though. There aren't any afternoon tours on match days. The café is open. You must try their famous strawberry cheesecake.

Anna: Where is the stadium? Can we get there by bus?

Receptionist: You can, it's Line 14 eastbound. But it's better to walk. The stadium's in East Melbourne, just a 10-minute walk from the city centre.

Ben: How can we get tickets for the match?

Receptionist: You can buy them at the ticket counter before the match. Or you book them online now. That's a little cheaper. The website is: mcg.org.au.

Anna and Ben: Thanks a lot for your help./Thanks.

Receptionist: You're welcome. Enjoy your day. Hope to see you later in the evening so you can tell me how you found the game ...

Hinweis: *Hier ergänzt du die fehlenden Angaben in der Tabelle. Die Informationen werden der Reihe nach im Hörtext erwähnt.*

Vokabelhinweise Tabelle (Aufgabenband Seite 2):

guided tour = geführte Tour
to include = beinhalten, einschließen
on match days = an Spieltagen
available = erhältlich

1. rugby
   Hinweis: *Z. 7*
2. Sydney
   Hinweis: *Z. 12 f.*
3. 5.45 (in the afternoon)
   Hinweis: *Z. 13*
4. changing rooms
   Hinweis: *Z. 16*
5. afternoon
   Hinweis: *Z. 17*
6. walk
   Hinweis: *Z. 21*
7. mcg.org.au
   Hinweis: *Z. 24*

B Use of English

Allgemeiner Hinweis: *In diesem Prüfungsteil liegt der Schwerpunkt auf Wortschatz und Grammatik.*

Aufgabe 1

Hinweis: *Im Lückentext musst du die vorgegebenen Wörter in die richtige Form bringen. Dabei kann es sich beispielsweise um die Zeitform eines Verbs oder die Steigerungsform eines Adjektivs handeln. Verändere nur das Wort in Klammern, aber auf keinen Fall den übrigen Satz.*

1. *took = Vergangenheitsform im „simple past": Die Reise nach Alice Springs fand bereits statt ("I went on a trip to Alice Springs.").*
2. *surprised = überrascht*
3. *largest = 2. Steigerungsform (Superlativ) des Adjektivs „large": „den größten Bestand von wilden Kamelen"*
4. *has never ridden = „present perfect": „Jemand, der noch nie auf einem Kamel geritten ist …"; im amerikanischen Englisch kann hier auch das „simple past" verwendet werden: „never rode"*
5. *sits = 3. Person Singular im „simple present": „der Reiter sitzt viel höher als auf einem Pferd"*
6. *slowly = Adverb: „bewegen sich langsam"*

7. *did not feel = verneinte Vergangenheitsform im „simple past": „Ich fühlte mich nicht unwohl ..."*

Like many other (0) **tourists** in Australia, I went on a trip to Alice Springs. There I (1) **took** the opportunity to ride a camel. I was (2) **surprised** to learn that there were camels in Australia but actually it has the (3) **largest** population of wild camels in the world. Someone who (4) **has never ridden** (BE)/**never rode** (AE) a camel before, may not know that the rider (5) **sits** much higher up than on a horse. Although camels usually move (6) **slowly**, they can also go faster than you might expect and then the rider is thrown backwards and forwards in the saddle.
I (7) **did not/didn't feel** bad on the back of my camel yesterday; it is an experience that I can recommend to everyone.

Aufgabe 2

Hinweis: *Finde jeweils ein passendes Wort, um die Textlücke sinnvoll zu ergänzen. Du kannst den unvollständigen Satz zunächst in deine Muttersprache übertragen und überlegen, welches Wort im Satzzusammenhang fehlt bzw. Sinn macht. Notiere anschließend das entsprechende englische Wort.*

1. *its = besitzanzeigendes Fürwort: „ein Sport, der seine Wurzeln auf Hawaii hat"; Vorsicht: hier besteht Verwechslungsgefahr mit „it's" = „es ist"*
2. *from = Präposition: „Surfer aus der ganzen Welt"*
3. *because/as/since = Konjunktion: „weil die Küste hervorragende Surfwellen bietet"; where = „nach Australien, wo die Küste hervorragende Surfwellen bietet"*
4. *feststehender Ausdruck „take place": stattfinden*
5. *„at a very young age" = „in sehr jungem Alter"*
6. *Zukunftsform mit „will": „Ich werde es versuchen"; das „going to-future" wäre zwar grammatikalisch auch richtig, ist hier aber nicht möglich, weil nur ein Wort pro Lücke eingesetzt werden darf.*

I've just arrived at the east coast (0) **where** impressive waves come crashing onto the beaches. Surfing is a very popular sport that has (1) **its** origins in Hawaii and which first came to Australia in 1915. Nowadays enthusiastic surfers (2) **from** around the world come to Australia (3) **because/as/since/where** the 50,000 km-long coast offers brilliant surfing waves. The oldest surfing competition in the world takes (4) **place** at Freshwater Beach and attracts over 7,000 competitors.
A lot of Australians start surfing (5) **at** a very young age, and tomorrow I (6) **will/shall** try it, too. I'm really looking forward to it.

Aufgabe 3

Hinweis: *Der Text enthält sieben Fehler aus den Bereichen Wortschatz und Grammatik. Jeder Fehler befindet sich immer in genau der Zeile, in der sich rechts daneben die nummerierte Linie für die Korrektur befindet.*

1. *starts (Grammatik): im „simple present" muss in der 3. Person Singular ein „s" angehängt werden*
2. *every (Wortschatz): every year = jedes Jahr*
   Vorsicht: Verwechslungsgefahr mit „all (the) year round" = ganzjährig
3. *sail (Grammatik): „simple present", da ausgedrückt wird, dass die Strecke jedes Jahr so verläuft*
4. *six and a half days (Wortschatz) = sechseinhalb Tage*
5. *events (Grammatik): Mehrzahl mit Plural-s = „one of the top events"*
6. *because/since/as/and (Wortschatz): „while" = „während" und passt hier somit nicht*
7. *sportsmen (Grammatik): die Mehrzahl (der Plural) von „man" ist „men"*

1.	starts	~~start~~
2.	every	~~all~~
3.	sail	~~sailed~~
4.	a	~~one~~
5.	events	~~event~~
6.	because / as / since / and	~~while~~
7.	sportsmen	~~sportsman~~

C Reading Comprehension

Allgemeiner Hinweis: *In diesem Prüfungsteil wird dein Leseverständnis geprüft, indem du Aufgaben zum allgemeinen und detaillierten Verständnis bearbeitest. Beim ersten Durchlesen gewinnst du einen Überblick, worum es im Text geht. Konzentriere dich beim zweiten Lesen darauf, den Inhalt möglichst genau zu verstehen. Dann beginnst du mit dem Aufgabenteil. Suche diejenigen Abschnitte oder Stellen im Text heraus, auf die sich die jeweilige Aufgabe bezieht. Vieles kannst du direkt aus dem Text als Antwort übernehmen, und auf diese Weise z. B. Rechtschreibfehler vermeiden.*

Vokabelhinweise:

Hier findest du eine Liste mit schwierigen Vokabeln aus dem Text. Zur Vorbereitung auf die Prüfung solltest du aber versuchen, möglichst viele Wörter aus dem Zusammenhang zu erschließen, sowie den Umgang mit dem Wörterbuch einzuüben. Aus

Zeitgründen kannst du in der schriftlichen Prüfung nur die Wörter nachschlagen, die du unbedingt zum Verständnis benötigst.

eco-friendly = umweltfreundlich
to sweep = fegen, kehren
Z. 4: environment = Umwelt
Z. 9: litter = Müll, Abfälle
Z. 10: rubbish = Abfall, Müll
*Z. 12: environmentalist = Umweltschützer*in*
Z. 12: movement = Bewegung
Z. 15: trash = Müll
Z. 15: to remain = bleiben
Z. 17: occasionally = gelegentlich
Z. 28: success = Erfolg
*Z. 28: founder = Gründer*in*
Z. 30: according to = laut (Angabe von)
Z. 38: to require = erfordern
Z. 38: instruction = Anleitung
Z. 38: equipment = Ausrüstung
Z. 40: suitable = geeignet, passend
Z. 40: to dispose = entsorgen
Z. 42: to decompose = sich zersetzen
Z. 52: most valuable asset = hier: wertvollstes Gut, größter Schatz
Z. 53: to carry on = weitermachen

Aufgabe 1

Hinweis: *Der Lesetext ist in die Absätze A bis F unterteilt (Beispiel: Absatz A = Zeile 1–11). Entscheide, in welchem Absatz die jeweilige Frage beantwortet wird. Beachte, dass die Frage den Inhalt betrifft, weshalb einzelne Wörter aus der Aufgabe nicht unbedingt wörtlich im Text vorkommen müssen.*

1. *Zeile 37 f.*
2. *Zeile 22 ff.*
3. *Zeile 45 f.*
4. *Zeile 12 f.*
5. *Zeile 28 f.*

0	1	2	3	4	5
A	E	C	F	B	C

Aufgabe 2

Hinweis: *Beantworte die Fragen in Stichpunkten oder in einem kurzen Satz. Es ist hilfreich, im Lesetext zunächst die Stelle zu markieren, die dir die Informationen zur Beantwortung der Frage liefert.*

Vokabelhinweise:
to keep clean = sauber halten
characteristic = Eigenschaft
to pick up = aufsammeln, aufheben

1. (by) bike
   Hinweis: *„cycle route to work" (Z. 14)*
2. (it) burns more calories / (the) pulse goes up and down / (it) trains (extra) muscles / extra muscles (are) used
   Hinweis: *Z. 30 ff.*
3. (they) wear/use gloves
   Hinweis: *Z. 39 f.*
4. (it) decomposes (extremely) slowly
   Hinweis: *Z. 42*
5. 6,400/6400 tons
   Hinweis: *Z. 48 f.*

Aufgabe 3

Hinweis: *Von den Aussagen a–j decken sich nur fünf mit dem Inhalt des Lesetextes. Vergleiche die Aussagen mit dem Inhalt des Textes, wähle die richtigen Aussagen und notiere diese.*

Vokabelhinweise:
to remove = entfernen
to collect = sammeln

(1) c
Hinweis: *Z. 15 f*

(2) d
Hinweis: *Z. 17 f.*

(3) g
Hinweis: *Z. 30 f.*

(4) i

Hinweis: *Z. 47 f.*

(5) j

Hinweis: *Z. 49 f.*

Aufgabe 4

Hinweis: *Ein Wort kann manchmal mehrere Bedeutungen haben. Dabei kommt es u. a. auf den Textzusammenhang an, aber auch darauf, ob das Wort z. B. als Nomen (Namenwort) oder Verb (Tunwort) verwendet wird oder Teil einer Redewendung ist. Bei dieser Aufgabe findest du – ähnlich wie in einem Wörterbuch – unterschiedliche, aber richtige Übersetzungen für das jeweilige englische Wort. Suche das Wort zunächst mithilfe der Zeilenangabe im Lesetext. Übersetze nun den entsprechenden Satz(teil), indem du die verschiedenen Bedeutungen verwendest. Auf diese Weise kannst du die richtige Übersetzung herausfinden.*

1. etw. entdecken

   Hinweis: *"whenever they spot a bottle, cup or any other litter" = „sobald sie eine Flasche, einen Becher oder irgendwelchen anderen Müll entdecken"*

2. sich ausbreiten

   Hinweis: *"since then the movement has spread around the world" = „seitdem hat sich diese Bewegung auf der ganzen Welt ausgebreitet"*

3. stehenbleiben

   Hinweis: *"When you run and stop repeatedly to pick up rubbish" = „wenn du immer wieder läufst und stehenbleibst um Müll aufzuheben"*

4. Art und Weise

   Hinweis: *"Everyone is allowed to do it in the way they want to" = „Alle können es auf die Art und Weise machen, wie sie möchten"*

5. Abfall

   Hinweis: *"there will probably be three times more plastic waste in the world's oceans" = „wahrscheinlich wird in den Weltmeeren dreimal so viel Plastikabfall sein"*

D Text Production

Allgemeiner Hinweis: *Lies dir beide Aufgabenstellungen erst einmal gut durch und entscheide dich dann entweder für die E-Mail oder für die Bildergeschichte. Berücksichtige die Vorgaben, die in der Aufgabenstellung enthalten sind. Achte auf einen klaren Satzbau, abwechslungsreichen Wortschatz sowie die Rechtschreibung. Verwende das Wörterbuch, und prüfe immer wieder, ob dein Text sprachlich richtig und inhaltlich schlüssig und verständlich ist. Du erhältst sowohl für den Inhalt als auch für die sprachliche Gestaltung Punkte. Halte dich an den vorgeschriebenen Umfang, schreibe leserlich und achte auf eine saubere äußere Form. Die folgenden Texte sind Lösungsbeispiele.*

Correspondence: E-Mail

Hinweis: *In der Aufgabenstellung wird zunächst die Schreibsituation erklärt. Es ist hilfreich, wenn du dir hier wichtige Informationen (z. B. E-Mail an das Hotel, Buchungsnummer) farblich markierst. Anschließend wird aufgezählt, welche Inhalte in deiner E-Mail vorkommen müssen. Halte dich an diese Angaben und achte darauf, alle Vorgaben in deiner E-Mail umzusetzen. Zusätzlich kannst du auch eigene passende Ideen notieren.*
Schreibe nun deinen Text. Die E-Mail geht an ein Hotel, d. h., dass ein formeller, höflicher Schreibstil erwartet wird. Achte deshalb auf eine angemessene Anrede. Da keine Kontaktperson genannt ist, kannst du „Dear Sir or Madam" schreiben. Verwende immer Langformen (z. B. „I am"). Reihe zudem nicht nur Stichpunkte aneinander, sondern schreibe immer ganze Sätze, die du nach Möglichkeit mit Konjunktionen (Bindewörtern) verbindest. Schlage unbekannte Vokabeln im Wörterbuch genau nach (z. B. „parking space/place" = Stellplatz für ein Auto, aber „car park/ parking lot" = gesamter Parkplatz).
Lies deine E-Mail am Ende noch einmal durch und überprüfe, ob dein Text leserlich und verständlich ist. Hake auf dem Angabenblatt die Inhalte ab, die du übernommen hast. Prüfe, ob du auf alle Punkte eingegangen bist. Eventuell kannst du inhaltlich auch noch etwas ausschmücken. Denke auch daran, dich unter Angabe deines Namens höflich zu verabschieden (z. B. „Yours faithfully", „Best regards"). Eine genaue Anleitung zum Schreiben einer E-Mail findest du übrigens im Kompetenzbereich „Schreiben" im Trainingsteil des Aufgabenbandes.

Dear Sir or Madam,

I am writing regarding my parents' booking (number XRN23125) from 2 May. Thank you for the booking confirmation and the extra information which you attached.

As an additional person is now going to come with us, I wanted to check with you if you have a single room or an extra bed (which we would prefer) available and how much it would cost.
I would also like to inform you that we will be checking in late on the day of our arrival. How can we obtain the room key if we arrive past 10 p.m.? We would also like to reserve a parking space if possible.
It would be grateful for your prompt reply.

Yours faithfully,

Isabel Seidl *(117 words)*

Creative Writing: Picture story

Hinweis: *In der Aufgabenstellung werden dir die Überschrift und der Einleitungssatz vorgegeben. Schreibe sie ab und setze die Geschichte passend fort. Betrachte die Bilder genau – auch Kleinigkeiten wie die Tüte, in der die Teenager von „Save the Ocean" den Müll einsammeln, oder der Gesichtsausdruck der Personen sind von Bedeutung. Denn so wird im letzten Bild klar, dass die Jugendlichen zum Schluss den Müll überreichen, den Trevor und Tammy am Strand zurückgelassen haben. In der Tüte befindet sich also kein Finderlohn!*
Gehe den Ablauf der Geschichte nun noch einmal durch und versuche, zu den Bildern jeweils passende Stichwörter zu finden, die du in deinen Text einbauen kannst (z. B. Bild 1: „beach", „food and drinks"; Bild 2: „evening", „go back to the hotel", „leave litter" etc.). Verfasse nun deine Geschichte in der Vergangenheitsform „simple past" (Last summer …). Schreibe in ganzen Sätzen und beachte die Satzstellung Subjekt – Verb – Objekt. Um die Geschichte auszuschmücken, kannst du z. B. die wörtliche Rede, Adjektive sowie Ort- und Zeitangaben verwenden. Überprüfe zum Schluss, ob deine Geschichte dem Umfang von ca. 100 Wörtern entspricht und auch dann verständlich ist, wenn man die Bilder nicht kennt. Eine genaue Anleitung zum Schreiben einer Bildergeschichte findest du im Kompetenzbereich „Text Production" im Trainingsteil des Aufgabenbandes.
Der folgende Text ist eine Beispiellösung. Er ist bewusst umfangreicher gehalten als in der Aufgabe gefordert. Dies soll dir Ideen für deine eigene Geschichte geben und es dir ermöglichen, deinen Wortschatz zu erweitern.

The lost key

Last summer Trevor and his girlfriend Tammy spent a day at the beach. They took drinks and food with them for a whole day: soda, chips, pizza, and so on. Tammy spent the day reading her magazine while Trevor sat under a parasol drinking soda.

When the couple went back to their hotel in the evening, they left a big mess: empty soda containers, a pizza box and a bag of chips.
Shortly afterwards, two teenagers called Charlie and Doug were collecting trash at the beach when they came to the place Trevor and Tammy had turned into a dump. "Whoa, what a mess!", Doug exclaimed and started to pick up the litter. "Look what I found" Charlie said, "A hotel key! It's from Paradise Hotel. I've got an idea ..."
Trevor and Tammy had just reported their lost room key at the hotel reception, when Charlie and Doug came into the lobby. They showed the key to the receptionist, who pointed at the couple. Charlie gave Tammy the key. The couple was happy to have it back, but Doug said: "Oh, one more thing – I believe you also left this", and he handed them a bag filled with the litter they had left at the beach. Tammy was really embarrassed and felt guilty. *(208 words)*

Notenschlüssel

Notenstufen	1	2	3	4	5	6
Punkte	80–68	67–55	54–41	40–27	26–13	12–0

Qualifizierender Abschluss der Mittelschule Bayern 2021
Lösungen – Englisch

A Listening Comprehension

Allgemeiner Hinweis: *Jeder Hörtext wird nacheinander zweimal abgespielt. Der Hörtext enthält zu Beginn sowie am Ende Pausen, um die zugehörigen Aufgaben zu lesen oder Lösungen zu korrigieren. Versuche während des Hörens schon möglichst viele Lösungen einzutragen.*

Aufgabe 1

Steve: Well, Sarah, tomorrow I'll show you my school. You'll be allowed to come to my lessons and meet all my friends. Later we'll go to my youth club. I usually meet some friends there to play darts.

Sarah: Aaaah, darts, I don't know about that. I've never been good at it. But what about the weekend? Can we go and see something special on Saturday?

Steve: Well, we could go to the cinema, or maybe the science museum. And there's the zoo of course, but we went there last time you were here, didn't we?

Sarah: Yes, we did. I liked it, but I thought we could visit somewhere special in the area maybe? Maybe a castle or something like that.

Steve: I'd love to take you to a football match, but Birmingham City are playing away from home this weekend. But what about going on a hiking tour in the Peak District?

Sarah: I know you're crazy about sports. But can't we do something I like, too?

Steve: You mean something like shopping? We do have a big shopping centre in South Birmingham. And after that we could go for a coffee.

Sarah: Ahh, wait a minute. Isn't there a famous chocolate factory around here? I read something about it in my guidebook.

Steve: Oh, you mean *Morrison's Chocolate World*? Yeah, we could go there. But it'll be a whole-day trip. It takes about an hour by bus to get there.

Sarah: Well, is it worth it?

Steve: Oh, yes. You can buy tickets on the company's website for about 25 pounds per person.

Sarah: Phew, well, that sounds a bit expensive.

Steve: Well, not really, everything is included: the bus ticket, a tour around the factory, and even a workshop. There you can create your own kind of chocolate.

Sarah: Well, that sounds good, and I hope we get to try lots of their products. I love *Morrison's* chocolate!

Steve: OK then, let's … let's go there on Saturday. But then you'll have to come hiking with me on Sunday.

Sarah: Oh, do I have to?

Steve: It'll do us good after all that chocolate …

Hinweis: *Du erhältst für jede richtige Lösung einen Punkt. Beantworte die Fragen kurz und knapp. Stichwörter in der jeweiligen Frage geben dir Hinweise, auf welche Stellen im Hörtext du besonders achten sollst. Die Antworten kommen im Hörtext in chronologischer Reihenfolge vor.*

1. football
   Hinweis: *Z. 10*
2. in South Birmingham
   Hinweis: *Z. 14 f.*
3. (about) one/an hour
   Hinweis: *Z. 19*
4. on the company's website/on the company's homepage/online/ on the internet
   Hinweis: *Z. 21*
5. (your) own (kind of) chocolate
   Hinweis: *Z. 25*
6. (go) hiking / hike
   Hinweis: *Z. 28 f.*

Aufgabe 2

Guide: Welcome to *Morrison's Chocolate World*. I'm Cathy and it's my pleasure to show you round the factory.
First, some facts about its history. Did you know that our company dates back to the year 1842? In that year, John Morrison opened a grocer's shop in Main Street Birmingham. Among other things he sold drinking chocolate, which he prepared himself.
The Morrison factory was founded in 1856, when Mr. Morrison bought a building in Crooked Street. This building is still the centre of our company today. By the year 1875 Morrison was selling 16 different kinds of drinking chocolate.
Since the end of the 19th century *Morrison's* has been selling chocolate in 100-gramme bars, the form that we are used to today. This chocolate tasted bitter by today's standards but it was something completely new at the time. Today the most popular kind of chocolate has milk in it and that's why it tastes sweeter.

The first section of the factory we visit is where we make our speciality: cream-filled eggs, which are made of two halves; milk chocolate on the outside and white and yellow cream on the inside. This makes the filling look like a real egg. The cream-filled eggs are our most popular product; we sell about 80 million of them in the United Kingdom every year.
The next section is the customer workshop, where people can use any of our ingredients to make up their own chocolate creations. It's great fun and people have some brilliant ideas. Sometimes these ideas even lead to new Morrison products. But we are not only interested in inventing new products. We are also trying to improve our existing ones, for example by making them healthier. Today our chocolate bars contain less sugar and no artificial flavouring at all. But the taste is just as good as ever. Now let's move on to …

Hinweis: *Die Sätze in der Aufgabe haben beinahe den gleichen Wortlaut wie im Hörtext. Höre genau hin, um das falsche Wort in der Aussage zu finden und durch das richtige aus dem Hörtext zu ersetzen. Falls dir das nicht gleich gelingt, versuche es beim zweiten Hören noch einmal.*

1. drinking
   Hinweis: *Z. 5; falsch: "… ~~milk~~ chocolate …"*
2. 1856
   Hinweis: *Z. 7; falsch: "… in ~~1865~~ …"*
3. bitter
   Hinweis: *Z. 11; falsch: "… tasted ~~sweet~~ …"*
4. cream (-filled)
   Hinweis: *Z. 14 f.; falsch: "… ~~chocolate~~-filled …"*
5. customer
   Hinweis: *Z. 19; falsch: "… ~~tourist~~ workshop …"*
6. healthier
   Hinweis: *Z. 22 f.; falsch: "… making them ~~tastier~~."*
7. less
   Hinweis: *Z. 24; falsch: "… ~~no~~ sugar …"*

Aufgabe 3

Employee: Hello, Birmingham Pizza Service, how can I help you?

Steve: Hi, I'd like to order two pizzas.

Employee: Which ones would you like?

Steve: I'd like two pizza margherita, but with some extra toppings. On the first one I'd like some bacon, onions and dried tomatoes. And for the second pizza: extra cheese and green peppers, please.

Employee: Well, you know that the green peppers are quite spicy.

Steve: Oh, then it's not a good idea I'll have some broccoli instead.

Employee: What about the size? Would you like small, regular or large?

Steve: The first pizza should be a large one, please. And pizza number two ... I think the medium size is big enough.

Employee: Anything else? How about a side salad? Or maybe a dessert? We've got apple pie or chocolate cake ...

Steve: Hm, that sounds good. We'll have two side salads. And for dessert: I don't think the chocolate cake is a good idea ... We'll both have the apple pie.

Employee: All right. Since you've chosen a side dish and a dessert, you get a free drink each. You can choose from mineral water, apple juice or lemonade.

Steve: Then we'll have two mineral waters, please. Er, no, hang on, I think I'd rather have an apple juice.

Employee: So that's one water and one apple juice. Is that all?

Steve: Yes, that's it.

Employee: Then I just need your details. Are you a regular customer?

Steve: I'm afraid not.

Employee: Then would you give me your name and address, please?

Steve: My name is Steve Johnson. I live at 5 Blackness Road.

Employee: And could I have a phone number, please? Just in case.

Steve: Of course, it's 524642 (Five-two-four-six-four-two).

Employee: Thank you. That'll be 22 pounds 80 altogether.

Steve: When can we expect the delivery?

Employee: In the next 30 minutes. It's 7.35 now. If your order hasn't arrived by 8.15 you'll get 5 pounds off your next order.

Steve: I see ... Thanks very much.

Employee: Let me just check your order. We've got two pizzas ...

Hinweis: *Folge dem Dialog und ergänze die fehlenden Angaben im Bestellformular. Die Wörter, die im Formular bereits vorgegeben sind, helfen dir bei der Orientierung im Hörtext und zeigen an, wann du mit dem nächsten fehlenden Wort rechnen kannst.*

1. onions
   Hinweis: *Z. 5*
2. cheese
   Hinweis: *Z. 6*
3. large
   Hinweis: *Z. 10*
4. apple pies
   Hinweis: *Z. 15*
5. (mineral) water
   Hinweis: *Z. 20*
6. 5/five
   Hinweis: *Z. 25*
7. 22.80/twenty-two eighty
   Hinweis: *Z. 28*

B Use of English

Allgemeiner Hinweis: *In diesem Prüfungsteil liegt der Schwerpunkt auf Wortschatz und Grammatik.*

Aufgabe 1

Hinweis: *Bei dieser Aufgabe musst du entscheiden, welches der vorgegebenen Wörter in die jeweilige Lücke passt. Achte dabei auf den Textzusammenhang und auch darauf, die Wörter aus der Vorgabe richtig abzuschreiben.*

1. *has become: Hier wird das „present perfect" verwendet, da es sich um einen Zeitraum („over recent years") handelt, der bis heute reicht.*
2. *end: Hier musst du die „simple present"-Form nehmen, da es hier um eine regelmäßige Handlung („every day") geht.*
3. *don't (feel comfortable): Auch hier steht das „simple present", passend zur Zeitform in der restlichen Satzhälfte („offer").*
4. *taken <u>to</u> a central collection point = <u>zu</u> einer zentralen Sammelstelle gebracht*
5. *Hier kann inhaltlich nur „<u>little</u> money" (= <u>wenig</u> Geld) passen.*

People have (0) **never** liked the idea of throwing food away.
Over recent years, wasting food (1) **has become** a "hot topic" again. Every day many tons of food (2) **end** up in rubbish containers. Fortunately, a group of people started to organise the collection of food which otherwise would be thrown away. Private people who (3) **don't** feel comfortable about wasting good food offer their "leftovers" – still unopened.
All this food is taken (4) **to** a central collection point, where some volunteers sort it out. They then give it to people who have (5) **little** money.
Today a growing number of people in need use this system on a regular basis.

Aufgabe 2

Hinweis: *Finde jeweils das Wort, das mit dem vorgegebenen Buchstaben beginnt und im Satzzusammenhang grammatikalisch und inhaltlich einen Sinn ergibt. Du darfst pro Lücke nur ein Wort einsetzen. Beachte auch die Rechtschreibung.*

1. *a new one = eine neue (Kaffeemaschine)*
2. *had the idea = hatte die Idee: „simple past", da das Ereignis bereits vergangen ist*
3. *equipment = Ausrüstung*
4. *place/point = Ort, Platz*
5. *what was going on = was passierte/geschah: „past progressive" (Verlaufsform in der Vergangenheit)*
6. *offer help to anybody/anyone = jeder/jedem Hilfe anbieten*
7. *need = brauchen: „simple present" (Signalwort „sometimes")*
8. *throwing them/things away = sie/Dinge wegwerfen*
9. *weight = Gewicht*
10. *environment = Umwelt*

Do you know what to do (0) **when** your coffee machine stops working?
Do you throw it away and buy a new (1) **one**?
You don't have to!
About twenty years ago some young student (2) **had** the idea of offering to repair other people's broken (3) **equipment**. A local café was a good (4) **place/point** to meet. When other people saw what (5) **was** going on, they joined in.
Now a large number of so-called "repair cafés" exist worldwide. They offer help to (6) **anybody/anyone** who asks for it. Sometimes their broken gadgets just (7) **need** a bit of cleaning, oiling or servicing. By repairing things instead of throwing (8) **them/things** away, we could save 350,000 kilos of rubbish year. This is equal to the (9) **weight** of about 58 fully grown African elephants. It is just a small contribution to protect our (10) **environment** but a step toward changing the world a little bit at a time.

Aufgabe 3

Hinweis: *Bei diesem Aufgabenformat findest du jeweils ein Wort in Klammern, das du so anpassen sollst, dass es grammatikalisch in den Satz passt. Dabei musst du das angegebene Wort z. B. in die Mehrzahl (den Plural) setzen oder die Wortart ändern und z. B. aus einem Substantiv ein Adjektiv machen. Beachte auch, dass du bei Verben die richtige Zeitform wählst.*

1. *a lot more than (Steigerung) = viel mehr als*
2. *have you ever heard of ...? (present perfect): hast du jemals von ... gehört?*
3. *production (Substantiv) = Produktion, Herstellung*
4. *dangerous (Adjektiv) = gefährlich*
5. *polish them regularly (Adverb): sie regelmäßig polieren*

What we usually know about vegetarians is that they avoid meat or other products from (0 animal) **animals**. But a vegetarian lifestyle means a lot (1 much) **more** than that. For example, have you ever (2 hear) **heard** of vegetarian shoes?
Instead of leather, wool, silk etc., synthetic materials have to be used for the (3 produce) **production** of vegetarian shoes. Synthetic materials are better because a lot of the processes for producing "animal leather" are bad for the environment and (4 danger) **dangerous** for the workers' health. Synthetics last longer and you can wash most of them in the washing machine. You cannot do that with your leather shoes, you need to wax and polish them (5 regular) **regularly**.
Unfortunately, these animal-friendly shoes are still quite expensive.

C Reading Comprehension

Allgemeiner Hinweis: *Die folgenden Aufgaben überprüfen, wie genau du den Lesetext verstanden hast. Verschaffe dir beim ersten Lesen einen Überblick über den Inhalt. Im Wörterbuch kannst du Begriffe nachschlagen, die du unbedingt zum Textverständnis brauchst. Gleiches gilt für Wörter, die in den Aufgaben vorkommen. Die Aufgaben werden dich immer wieder auf bestimmte Stellen im Lesetext lenken, die du nochmals genau durchgehen solltest, bevor du die Antwort notierst. Es kann hilfreich sein, wenn du dir bestimmte Textstellen farblich markierst.*

Vokabelhinweise:
Hier findest du eine Liste mit schwierigen Vokabeln aus dem Text. Zur Vorbereitung auf die Prüfung solltest du aber versuchen, möglichst viele Wörter aus dem Zusammenhang zu erschließen, sowie den Umgang mit dem Wörterbuch einzuüben. Aus Zeitgründen kannst du in der schriftlichen Prüfung nur die Wörter nachschlagen, die du unbedingt zum Verständnis benötigst.

Z. 5: plant-based: pflanzlich
Z. 23: mock meat: Fleischersatz
Z. 33: blood pressure: Blutdruck
Z. 41: nutrition facts: Nährwertangaben
Z. 47: dairy products: Milchprodukte
Z. 51: wholemeal products: Vollkornprodukte

Aufgabe 1

Hinweis: *Ordne die vorgegebenen Überschriften (1–8) den Abschnitten im Lesetext (A–G) zu. Zwei Überschriften passen zu keinem Abschnitt.*

B	C	D	E	F	G
7	**6**	**8**	**4**	**5**	**3**

Aufgabe 2

Hinweis: *Bei dieser Aufgabe werden dir fünf Fragen gestellt. Die Antwort auf jede Frage findest du immer in einem bestimmten Abschnitt des Lesetextes (A–G). Notiere im jeweiligen Kästchen den passenden Absatz.*
Vokabelhinweise: amount: Menge, to dine: essen

1. there is a country where the state helps to inform customers about vegetarian foods? **E**
2. more and more consumers want to reduce the amount of meat they eat? **F**
3. some people who go out and dine meat-free do not expect it to be as nice as it is? **A**
4. the decision to avoid eating meat can be a matter of belief? **C**
5. some vegetarian foods look and taste almost the same as popular meat dishes? **D**

Aufgabe 3

Hinweis: *Wie in einem Wörterbuch findest du hier verschiedene Übersetzungen zu einem englischen Wort. Lies den ganzen zugehörigen Satz im Text genau durch und entscheide dann, welche Wortbedeutung im Textzusammenhang inhaltlich und grammatikalisch Sinn ergibt.*

1. sättigend
2. trotzdem
3. Kennzeichnung
4. Ernährung
5. überprüfen

Aufgabe 4

Hinweis: *Hier werden dir zehn Aussagen („statements") vorgelegt, die du mit dem Text vergleichen sollst. Nur vier dieser Aussagen stimmen mit dem Text überein. Diese Aufgabe ist nicht ganz einfach, da die Aussagen anders formuliert sind als im Lesetext und du sowohl die „statements" als auch die Informationen im Text genau verstehen musst. Die richtigen Aussagen findest du an folgenden Stellen im Text:*
statement 4: Z. 30 f.
statement 6: Z. 33
statement 9: Z. 40 ff.
statement 10: Z. 50

True statements: 4, 6, 9, 10

D Text Production

Allgemeiner Hinweis: *Lies dir beide Aufgabenstellungen erst einmal gut durch und entscheide dich dann entweder für die E-Mail oder für die Bildergeschichte. Berücksichtige die Vorgaben, die in der Aufgabenstellung enthalten sind. Achte auf einen klaren Satzbau, abwechslungsreichen Wortschatz sowie die Rechtschreibung. Verwende das Wörterbuch, und prüfe immer wieder, ob dein Text sprachlich richtig und inhaltlich schlüssig und verständlich ist. Du erhältst sowohl für den Inhalt als auch für die sprachliche Gestaltung Punkte. Halte dich an den vorgeschriebenen Umfang, schreibe leserlich und achte auf eine saubere äußere Form. Die folgenden Texte sind Lösungsbeispiele.*

Hinweis: *In der Aufgabe wird zunächst die Schreibsituation erklärt. Zudem ist aufgelistet, welche Inhalte dein Brief enthalten muss. Es ist wichtig, dass du all diese Vorgaben in deinem Text unterbringst. Gerne kannst du deine Fanpost auch noch durch eigene Ideen ergänzen.*
Schreibe in ganzen Sätzen. Wörter, die du für deinen Text brauchst, kannst du im Wörterbuch nachschlagen. Lies den Brief am Ende noch einmal durch und überprüfe, ob dein Text leserlich und verständlich ist und ob du an Datum, Anrede und Schlussformel gedacht hast. Hake in der Angabe alle Vorgaben ab, die du in deinem Brief umgesetzt hast und ergänze fehlende Inhalte. Eine genaue Anleitung zum Schreiben eines Briefs findest du übrigens im Kompetenzbereich „Schreiben" im Trainingsteil des Aufgabenbandes.

30 July 20xx

Dear Zoe,

I'm Emma, a 15-year-old student from Germany. I've been a big fan of yours since I heard your song "Caress" last year. The song is great – I have listened to it so many times and I also sing it myself!
I absolutely love your music and your style. When I'm listening to your songs, I really feel that they come from your heart. Last month, I went to one of your concerts and I was really impressed by your performance!
Now I'd like to ask you if I could have two autographs – one for me and one for my friend Stefanie, who is also a big fan of yours. I enclose an envelope and stamps so that you can send me the autographs without any cost.
Thank you so much!

Love,
Emma *(135 words)*

Hinweis: *In der Aufgabenstellung werden dir die Überschrift und der Beginn der Geschichte vorgegeben. Schreibe sie ab und setze die Geschichte passend fort. Betrachte das Bild genau und lies auch die Stichwörter in den Kästchen, die dir verbindliche Hinweise zum Handlungsverlauf geben.*
Verfasse nun deine Geschichte im „simple past" (Last summer the parcel service rang …). Schreibe in ganzen Sätzen und versuche, diese mit Konjunktionen (Bindewörtern) zu verbinden. Um die Geschichte auszuschmücken, kannst du z. B. die wörtliche Rede und Adjektive verwenden. Überprüfe zum Schluss, ob deine Geschichte dem vorgegebenen Umfang entspricht und auch dann verständlich ist, wenn man das Bild und die Vorgaben nicht kennt. Eine genaue Anleitung zum Schreiben einer Bildergeschichte findest du im Kompetenzbereich „Schreiben" im Trainingsteil des Aufgabenbandes. Der folgende Text ist eine Beispiellösung.

Cat on tour

Last summer the parcel service rang at the Millers' house. While the driver was delivering the parcel to Mr and Mrs Miller, Joe, the Millers' cat, slipped through the open door. It had heard a noise coming from inside the driver's truck and jumped into the vehicle, hoping to catch a mouse. When the driver returned to his truck, he closed the back door with a bang: now Joe was caught inside and there wasn't even a mouse to catch!
The driver started his truck and began to sing to some music on the radio. Suddenly, he heard a couple of loud meows. That was when he noticed the cat in the truck and figured that it belonged to the Millers. While he was driving back to their house, Joe and the driver continued to "sing" together, which both of them enjoyed. In the end, the Millers were very glad to get another delivery that day!

(146 words)

Notenschlüssel

Notenstufen	1	2	3	4	5	6
Punkte	80–68	67,5–55	54,5–41	40,5–27	26,5–13	12,5–0

Qualifizierender Abschluss der Mittelschule Bayern 2022
Lösungen – Englisch

A Hör- und Hörsehverstehen

Allgemeiner Hinweis: *Die Aufgaben folgen dem Aufbau des Hörtextes. Somit können sie der Reihe nach beantwortet werden. In diesem Prüfungsteil darf ein zweisprachiges Wörterbuch (in Printform) verwendet werden. Nutze es in den Textpausen. Wenn der Text abgespielt wird, solltest du dich jedoch nur auf das Hören konzentrieren.*

Task 1

Meredith: I'm so excited to be here in New York. Where shall we go first?

Ben: No idea. There's so much to do here. There are hundreds of sights in New York.

Meredith: All those famous buildings ... and what about Central Park? And shopping on Fifth Avenue? And I definitely want to see a show on Broadway. I love going to the theater.

Ben: Is Broadway a famous theater?

Meredith: Actually, Broadway is a long street in Manhattan, just off Times Square, which is famous for its theaters.

Ben: Ah, yes, there was something in my guidebook ... Mhm ... there are more than 40 theaters on Broadway.

Meredith: Plenty of choice then.

Ben: The guidebook says that you should always book tickets in advance because the shows are often sold out.

Meredith: It's too late for that then.

Ben: But ... there's a ticket counter at Times Square that sells last-minute tickets for all Broadway shows.

Meredith: Let's go there first, then. Look, I just found something else on the Internet. It's called the New York Pass.

Ben: What's that?

Meredith: It's a special ticket that gives you free entry to over a hundred tourist attractions.

Ben: That sounds useful. I'd like to see the Empire State Building, the Statue of Liberty and the Museum of Modern Art.

Meredith: Well ... They're all included here, even a bus tour and the ferry to Ellis Island.

Ben: How much is it?

Meredith: Well, you can buy the pass for as many days as you want. It's 204 dollars per person for three days.

Ben: That's quite a lot.

Meredith: Yes, but it would be more expensive to pay for each tourist attraction separately. The Empire State Building alone costs 42 dollars each.

Ben: OK, how do we get this New York Pass? Can you buy it in stores?

Meredith: You can, but it's cheaper and more practical to download it onto our phones. The scanner at the entrance reads it and we can simply go in. We don't even have to wait in line.

Ben: Super! So, let's do that. And then let's try the ticket counter on Times Square.

Meredith: Yes, but don't forget my shopping trip …

Hinweis: *Ergänze die fehlenden Details in der Tabelle mithilfe des Hörtextes. Achte auf die Schlüsselbegriffe in der linken Spalte der Tabelle (z. B. „Broadway"). Diese kommen auch im Hörtext vor und signalisieren, dass die benötigten Informationen nun folgen.*

1. (long) street
   Hinweis: *Z. 8*
2. 40/forty
   Hinweis: *Z. 11*
3. last-minute
   Hinweis: *Z. 16 f.*
4. free entry
   Hinweis: *Z. 19 ff.*
5. bus tour
   Hinweis: *Z. 25 f.*
6. three days
   Hinweis: *Z. 28 f.*
7. cheaper
   Hinweis: *Z. 34*

Task 2

Meredith: Good morning, we would like to ask about last-minute tickets for shows tonight or tomorrow night. Are there any left?

Anne: Well, do you want to see a musical or a play?

Meredith: We would prefer a musical.

Anne: There are tickets left for three musicals: Lion King, Wicked and Mrs. Doubtfire.

Meredith: Well, I've already seen Wicked, so it's Mrs Doubtfire or Lion King.

Ben: Aah, I'm not so interested in Mrs Doubtfire.

Meredith: Fine. Let's watch Lion King then. Is it any good?

Anne: It's a very popular show. And, it's showing at Hamilton Theater. That's one of the nicest theaters on Broadway.

Ben: And where exactly is it?

Anne: Most theaters on Broadway are within walking distance from here. But Hamilton Theater is a bit further north, west of Central Park.

Meredith: OK, so it's too far to walk. But how do we get there?

Anne: If you don't want to walk, you can always take the subway. Or a cab.

Ben: OK. And when does the show start tonight?

Anne: I'm sorry, but the only tickets left for Lion King are for tomorrow's show. It's sold out tonight. But there are two shows tomorrow, at 5 and at 8.30 pm.

Meredith: 5 is too early. So it's 8.30.

Ben: Yes, definitely.

Anne: Excellent. Let's see … I've got some seats on the ground floor or upstairs. Where do you want to sit?

Ben: Upstairs seats are probably nicer, aren't they?

Anne: They are, but they are much more expensive. And at Hamilton Theater, the ground floor seats are also very nice.

Meredith: Ground floor then. How much are the tickets there?

Anne: 45 dollars each. I'm afraid we only accept credit cards.

Ben: No problem. Here's my card.

Anne: Thank you. And your tickets … By the way, make sure that you're on time. The doors close ten minutes before the show starts.

Meredith: Thank you very much.

Ben: Thanks, bye.

Meredith: Goodbye.

Anne: Bye.

Ben: That's great. Now, we have time to go to Madison Square Garden tonight.

Hinweis: *Beantworte die Fragen in Stichpunkten. Achte genau auf die verwendeten Fragewörter („where" = „wo", „how" = „wie", „which" = „welche") und unterstreiche in der Aufgabe die Schlüsselwörter (z. B. Hamilton Theater). Sobald du ein Schlüsselwort im Hörtext erkennst, kannst du damit rechnen, dass die gesuchten Informationen unmittelbar folgen werden.*

1. (a bit) (further) north, west of Central Park
   Hinweis: *Z. 14*
2. subway / cab / walk
   Hinweis: *Z. 16*
3. (the show at) 8.30 (pm)
   Hinweis: *Z. 20*
4. ground floor (seats)
   Hinweis: *Z. 27*
5. (by) (credit) card
   Hinweis: *Z. 28 f.*

Task 3

Marc: Welcome to Madison Square Garden, the world's most famous arena. During our 75-minute tour you'll visit the backstage area, learn about the history of the arena and have a go at our interactive stations. There you can, for example, compare the size of your hand to that of a professional basketball player.

Madison Square Garden, or simply 'the Garden', as New Yorkers call it, first opened in 1879 and has been a center for entertainment ever since. It was named after James Madison, the fourth president of the United States. The present building, the fourth construction of the Garden, was opened in 1968. It is home of the Knicks, New York's basketball team, and also of the Rangers, our ice-hockey team. How is that possible, you ask? It's quite simple: The floor of the arena has to be changed for each sport: It is either a wooden basketball court or an ice-rink. Our staff can manage this change within three and a half hours. Fortunately, this is only necessary three or four times a year, when basketball and ice-hockey matches are played on the same day.

The Garden was also the location for one of the greatest boxing events in history: In 1971, 20 000 fans watched Joe Frazier win his fight against Muhammad Ali. This is still known as 'The Fight of the Century'.

Another highlight in the Garden's history was Michael Jordan's first game here. He scored 33 points for his team, the Chicago Bulls, against the Knicks. It was the first of many great performances by Jordan here.

But Madison Square Garden is not only a sports arena. It is also used for rock concerts and comedy shows. Next month, two celebrities will be playing here. If you are interested, there are still a few hundred tickets left for the event.

Hinweis: *Folge dem Hörtext aufmerksam und wähle dann in der Aufgabe das jeweils korrekte Satzende aus. Beachte, dass die Satzanfänge im Hörtext nicht exakt so vorkommen, wie sie in der Aufgabe stehen, sondern in etwas anderer Form. Die Schlüsselwörter in der Aufgabe (z. B. „interactive station") helfen dir, die zugehörige Stelle im Hörtext zu erkennen.*

1. compare your hand with a professional's.
   Hinweis: *Z. 3 f.*
2. entertainment since 1879.
   Hinweis: *Z. 5 f.*
3. former president.
   Hinweis: *Z. 6 f.*
4. change the floor.
   Hinweis: *Z. 10 ff.*
5. 'The Fight of the Century'.
   Hinweis: *Z. 17*
6. Michael Jordan's first game.
   Hinweis: *Z. 18*

B Sprachgebrauch

Allgemeiner Hinweis: *In diesem Prüfungsteil liegt der Schwerpunkt auf Wortschatz und Grammatik. Du darfst ein zweisprachiges Wörterbuch (in Printform) verwenden. Verwende es auch, um deine Rechtschreibung zu überprüfen, da ein falsch geschriebenes Wort zu Punktverlust führt.*

Aufgabe 1

Hinweis: *Lies den Lückentext zunächst einmal ganz durch, um dir einen Überblick zu verschaffen. Der Text darf bei der Bearbeitung nicht verändert werden. Ergänze die Lücke, indem du ein passendes Wort findest, das inhaltlich und sprachlich passt. Das Wörterbuch kann dabei hilfreich sein.*

(1) Die Lücke bezieht sich auf „tracks" („die Gleise"), also muss das Personalpronomen Plural stehen („they").

(4) Beachte den Unterschied in der Bedeutung von „those" („jene") und „these" („diese").

(6) Wenn du ein Adjektiv steigerst, das aus drei Silben besteht („beau-ti-ful"), verwende den Superlativ mit „most".

New York City has (0) **one** of the biggest systems of underground trains in the world. If somebody put all the tracks end to end, (1) **they** would reach from New York to Chicago.

The subway never closes completely, some trains run twenty-four hours, seven days (2) **a** week, all year round.

Entrances with red-ball signs are closed (3) **at/every/all** night, while (4) **those/others/entrances** with green-ball signs are open 24/7.

The subway in New York is the busiest in the US but Tokyo in Japan (5) **has/transports/carries** twice as many passengers a year. As well as being one of the world's oldest and busiest systems, New York City's subway has a number of well-kept secrets. Here are two of them. City Hall subway station is one of the (6) **most/really** beautiful sections of the subway but it is no longer in use. The nicely decorated walls and elegant windows make it (7) **look/appear/seem** like a little church. This is not a surprise because the architects also designed the Cathedral of St. John the Divine. The other secret lies below a famous hotel which has its own special station only for VIPs. Once an American president used it to (8) **hide/disguise** the fact that he needed a wheelchair. Nowadays, the station is still used as an emergency escape when presidents stay in the hotel above.

Hinweis: *Bei dieser Aufgabe musst du die in Klammern angegebenen Wörter jeweils so anpassen, dass die Sätze sinnvoll und sprachlich richtig vervollständigt werden. Dies geschieht, indem du z. B. aus einem Verb ein Nomen machst (z. B. „build" → „building"). Beachte, dass das Wort aus der derselben Wortfamilie stammen muss wie das vorgegebene Wort in Klammern. Es darf also kein völlig anderes Wort sein (z. B. „high" – „tall"). Beachte, dass du bei Verben manchmal einfach nur die Zeitform ändern musst (z. B. bei „to be" → „was"/„were", „has been", „had been"). Verwende bei Bedarf das Wörterbuch, um das gesuchte Wort nachzuschlagen oder die Rechtschreibung zu kontrollieren.*

1. *height = Höhe*
2. *fifth (Avenue) = fünfte (Straße)*
3. *Setze das Verb ins „simple past", weil das Ereignis bereits in der Vergangenheit stattfand und abgeschlossen ist. Verwende die Plural-Form „were", da das Verb sich auf „plans" bezieht.*
4. *successful = erfolgreich*
5. *leading (role) = führende (Rolle)*
6. *signed/had signed („unterschrieb"/„hatte unterschrieben"): Der Satz bezieht sich weiterhin auf die Vergangenheit, daher muss das „simple past" verwendet werden, aber auch das „past perfect" ist möglich.*
7. *came up with: weiterhin „simple past"*
8. *painter = Maler/Malerin; wie auch „sculptors" muss „painters" im Plural stehen*
9. *has become: „present-perfect" mit Signalwörter „over the years" – über die Jahre (bis heute) wurde das Rockefeller Center zu einer Attraktion, die man gesehen haben muss.*
10. *attraction = Attraktion, Sehenswürdigkeit*

The Rockefeller Center – a complex of about 20 (0 build) **buildings** – lies in the center of Manhattan. The Comcast Building – one of the 19 skyscrapers – is the tallest building with a (1 high) **height** of 259 m. The Rockefeller Center is situated near (2 five) **Fifth/fifth/5th** Avenue. Back in 1926 there (3 be) **were** plans to create a new opera house. John Rockefeller – a (4 success) **successful** businessman – liked the architect's concept so much that he took a (5 lead) **leading** role in the project. He himself (6 signature) **signed/had signed** a contract to rent the land for 24 years. After the 1929 financial crash, the opera house owners didn't want to be part of the project anymore. So, Rockefeller had to think of something different and he (7 come) **came** up with the idea of constructing 'a city within a city' – both a commercial and a cultural center. The concept was totally new. He built a group of skyscrapers as one unit and integrated art works from well-known sculptors and (8 paint) **painters**.

Over the years the Rockefeller Center (9 become) **has become** a must-see sight for visitors. The ice-skating rink in front of the Rockefeller Center is visited by half a million people every year, especially when the impressively decorated Christmas tree is to be seen.

Another (10 attract) **attraction** is the Rainbow Restaurant on the 65th floor. It offers delicious food and a beautiful view over the city.

C Leseverstehen

Allgemeiner Hinweis: *Die folgenden Aufgaben überprüfen, wie genau du den Lesetext verstanden hast. Verschaffe dir beim ersten Lesen einen Überblick über den Inhalt. Die Aufgaben werden dich immer wieder auf bestimmte Stellen im Lesetext lenken, die du nochmal genau durchgehen solltest, bevor du deine Antwort notierst. Es kann hilfreich sein, wenn du dir bestimmte Textstellen farblich markierst.*

Vokabelhinweise:
Hier findest du eine Liste mit schwierigen Vokabeln aus dem Text. Zur Vorbereitung auf die Prüfung solltest du aber versuchen, möglichst viele Wörter aus dem Zusammenhang zu erschließen, sowie den Umgang mit dem Wörterbuch einzuüben. Aus Zeitgründen kannst du in der schriftlichen Prüfung nur die Wörter nachschlagen, die du unbedingt zum Verständnis benötigst.

Z. 1 f.: skyscraper = Wolkenkratzer
Z. 18 f.: disappointed = enttäuscht
Z. 29: ferry = Fähre
Z. 37: observation deck = Aussichtsplattform
Z. 40: subway = U-Bahn
Z. 45: experience = Erfahrung

Aufgabe 1

Hinweis: *Suche jeweils die Stelle im Text, die zu den Satzanfängen passt. Lies nach und kreuze die richtige Antwort an.*

1. in a café.
   Hinweis: *Z. 12 f.*
2. street food.
   Hinweis: *Z. 19 ff.*
3. Empire State Building.
   Hinweis: *Z. 17 f. und Z. 22 f.*

4. experience the atmosphere.
   Hinweis: *Z. 33 ff.*

Aufgabe 2

Hinweis: *Lies die Fragen sorgfältig durch und kläre unbekannte Wörter mithilfe des Wörterbuchs. Suche anschließend die zugehörigen Textstellen. Schreibe in deiner Antwort nicht den kompletten Satz aus dem Text ab, sondern notiere nur die Informationen, die die Frage genau beantworten. Beachte auch die Rechtschreibung.*

1. 4/four hours
   Hinweis: *Z. 7*
2. (because) (it was) close to the coolest places (in Manhattan)
   Hinweis: *Z. 10 f.*
3. (it was) cold/windy
   Hinweis: *Z. 18; unpleasant = unangenehm, ungemütlich*
4. shopping
   Hinweis: *Z. 29 f.*
5. (the) Rockefeller Center
   Hinweis: *Z. 36 ff.; fabulous = fabelhaft, wunderbar; the whole city = die ganze Stadt*

Aufgabe 3

Hinweis: *Du findest in dieser Aufgabe fünf Fragen. Jede Frage wird im Lesetext in einem bestimmten Absatz (A–G) beantwortet. Ordne den richtigen Absatz der Frage zu. Beachte, dass im Text nicht genau die gleichen Wörter wie in der Frage verwendet werden. Beispiel: „public transport" (in Frage 1), aber „subway" im Lesetext.*

Which paragraph tells the reader that …

1.	using public transport in New York can be exciting and interesting?	F
2.	the girls had dinner at an elegant place?	E
3.	the girls are still waiting for their plan for the future to become reality?	G

4. they used an old-fashioned way to get around a popular part of Manhattan? **E**

5. they realized for the first time that they were finally in the city of their dreams? **C**

Aufgabe 4

Hinweis: *Wie in einem Wörterbuch findest du hier verschiedene Übersetzungen für ein englisches Wort. Lies den ganzen dazugehörigen Satz im Text genau durch und entscheide, welche Wortbedeutung im Textzusammenhang inhaltlich und grammatikalisch Sinn ergibt.*

1. dennoch
2. allzu
3. ungefähr
4. nennen

D Sprachmittlung

Allgemeiner Hinweis: *Auf Grundlage des Foodblogs sollst du einen zusammenhängenden Text* <u>*auf Deutsch*</u> *verfassen. Deine E-Mail sollte auf die beiden Empfänger*innen zugeschnitten sein, etwa 80 Wörter umfassen und in vollständigen Sätzen geschrieben sein. Lies dir die Aufgabe zunächst durch und markiere wichtige Hinweise zur Bearbeitung farbig. Gehe dann den Blog durch. Schlage unbekannte Wörter, die du nicht aus dem Textzusammenhang klären kannst, im Wörterbuch nach. Du wirst bestimmte Textstellen nochmals lesen müssen, bevor du diese sinngemäß ins Deutsche überträgst. Beachte auf jeden Fall folgende Punkte:*

- *Du schreibst eine persönliche E-Mail an deine Bekannten Chris und Kim.*
- *Schlage* <u>*jeweils*</u> <u>*ein*</u> *Essen für Chris und Kim vor (es gibt mehrere passende Speisen zur Auswahl).*
- *Da Kim nichts Süßes mag, empfiehlst du ihr/ihm den Bagel oder den Shushi-Donut; Chris würdest du die süßen „Bubble Waffles" oder die Eiscreme aus Yams empfehlen.*
- *Begründe deine Wahl, indem du jede Speise, die du ausgewählt hast, genauer beschreibst.*

Hi,

im Internet bin ich auf einen tollen Foodblog gestoßen. Ich denke, da wäre auch für euch etwas dabei. Für Chris empfehle ich „Bubble Waffles". Das sind Waffeln, die außen knusprig und innen weich sind. Sie sind wie Eiswaffeln geformt und mit Speiseeis unterschiedlicher Geschmacksrichtungen gefüllt. Außerdem können sie mit allem Möglichem ergänzt werden, zum Beispiel mit Früchten, Keksen oder süßen Soßen. Alternativ gäbe es für Chris als Eisliebhaber eine lila Eiscreme, die aus Yams derselben Farbe hergestellt wird, aber trotzdem süß schmeckt.
Kim würde ich den „Sushi-Donut" empfehlen. Dieser wird aus Reis gemacht und kann durch alles Mögliche aufgepeppt werden, wie zum Beispiel Lachs, Avocado, Gurke oder Mango. Viel Spaß in New York!

Lasst's euch schmecken ☺

Liebe Grüße

E Text- und Medienkompetenzen

Allgemeiner Hinweis: *Zu dieser Aufgabe findest du einen Chatverlauf. Verwende die Informationen daraus, um anschließend das Buchungsformular auf Englisch auszufüllen. Lies sowohl den Chat als auch die Aufgabe gründlich durch, und schlage unbekannte Wörter im Wörterbuch nach. Beachte, dass du im unteren Teil des Formulars in ganzen Sätzen antworten musst – Stichpunkte führen zu Punktverlust.*

Central Hostel					
City	New York				
First name	**Lindsey**		Last name	**Smith**	
Number of guests	[2] adults		[ ] children		
Room category	[ ] single room		[✓] double room	[ ] family room	
Check-in date	**May 2nd**		Length of stay	**14 days/ fortnight**	

Do you have any special requests?
• **We need two single beds, not a double bed.** • **Please give us a bedroom with its own bathroom.** • **We would like to have breakfast in the hostel.** • **One breakfast needs to be vegan.** • **If possible, please provide transfer from the airport to the hostel. We will arrive at night.** • **We would like to store our valuables in a locker.**

F Schreiben

Correspondence: E-Mail

Hinweis: *Schreibe eine E-Mail auf Englisch, in der du dich auf die Stelle als Babysitter*in bei einer amerikanischen Familie bewirbst. Alle Inhaltspunkte, die in der Aufgabe aufgelistet sind, müssen in deiner E-Mail vorkommen. Hake sie während des Schreibens der Reihe nach ab, sobald du darauf eingegangen bist. Gerne kannst du deinen Text auch noch mit eigenen Ideen ausschmücken.*
Denke an eine höfliche Anrede zu Beginn der E-Mail und die passende Schlussformel. Da es sich um eine eher formelle E-Mail handelt, solltest du Langformen (z. B. „I am", „I would like to …") verwenden. Tipps und Hinweise zum Schreiben einer E-Mail findest du im Kompetenzbereich „Schreiben" im Trainingsteil des Aufgabenbandes. Der folgende Text ist eine Beispiellösung.

Dear Robertson family,

I found your ad in our daily newspaper and would be interested to work as your babysitter. Next year I will take my final exams, and although my English is quite good I would like to improve it.
I am 15 years old and as a hobby I play the bass guitar in a band. One day I would like to become a professional musician.
I think I am suited for the job because I have a younger sister and brother who I take care of while my parents are at work. They usually have long working hours because they own a restaurant.
I would be interested to learn how many children you have and how old they are. Where do you live and what would my working hours be? How much would I earn per hour/day?

I hope to hear from you soon.

Yours sincerely,
(your name) *(149 words)*

Creative Writing: Picture story

Hinweis: *In der Aufgabenstellung werden dir die Überschrift und der Beginn der Geschichte vorgegeben. Schreibe sie ab und setze die Geschichte passend fort. Betrachte die Bilder genau und versuche zu erkennen, was auf ihnen dargestellt wird. Verfasse nun deine Geschichte im „simple past" ("Last summer Alex and some friends went on a hiking tour ..."). Schreibe in ganzen Sätzen und versuche, diese mit Konjunktionen (Bindewörtern) zu verbinden. Um die Geschichte auszuschmücken, kannst du z. B. die wörtliche Rede und Adjektive verwenden. Überprüfe zum Schluss, ob deine Geschichte dem vorgegebenen Umfang entspricht und auch dann verständlich ist, wenn man die Bilder nicht kennt. Eine genaue Anleitung zum Schreiben einer Bildergeschichte findest du im Kompetenzbereich „Schreiben" im Trainingsteil des Aufgabenbandes. Der folgende Text ist eine Beispiellösung.*

Best lunch ever

Last summer Alex and some friends went on a hiking tour. In the morning Alex was late packing his things. His friends Carla, Mike, Jenny and Jane were impatiently waiting for him at his door, so Alex had to hurry up, forgetting his lunchbox, his banana and water bottle on the table. "I'm coming!" he yelled as he hurried to the door.

It was a long hike uphill until Alex and his friends finally reached a place where they could rest and have a picnic. His friends had brought along blankets which they spread on the ground underneath two old trees. When Alex was unpacking his backpack, he realized that he had left his snacks at home. "Oh silly me!" he exclaimed. "What am I going to eat now?" "Don't worry! Here's a bottle of soda for you," said Carla and right away Mike added "I could share a sandwich with you". Then Jenny passed him an apple and smiled.

"Wow, you're such nice friends. This is the best lunch ever!" Alex said with relief.

(161 words)

Notenschlüssel

Notenstufen	1	2	3	4	5	6
Punkte	92,0–78,0	77,5–63,0	62,5–47	46,5–31	30,5–16	15,5–0

Qualifizierender Abschluss der Mittelschule Bayern 2023
Lösungen – Englisch

Um dir die Lösungen zur Prüfung 2023 schnellstmöglich zur Verfügung stellen zu können, bringen wir sie in digitaler Form heraus.

Sobald die Original-Prüfungsaufgaben 2023 freigegeben sind, können die dazugehörigen Lösungen als PDF auf der Plattform **MyStark** heruntergeladen werden. Deinen persönlichen Zugangscode findest du auf der Umschlaginnenseite vorne im Buch.

Aktuelle Prüfung

www.stark-verlag.de/mystark